accidentally ME

a novel by
Kim Karras

Published by Sweetwater Books
An imprint of Cedar Fort, Inc.
Springville, Utah

ISBN 13: 978-1-4621-1867-0

Published by Sweetwater Books, an imprint of Cedar Fort, Inc.
2373 W. 700 S., Springville, UT, 84663
Distributed by Cedar Fort, Inc., www.cedarfort.com

LIBRARY OF CONGRESS CATALOGING-IN-PUBLICATION DATA

Names: Karras, Kim, 1980- author.
Title: Accidentally me / Kim Karras.
Description: Springville, Utah : Sweetwater Books, an imprint of Cedar Fort, Inc., [2016] | Summary: When perfect daughter Sabrina learns that her parents only have enough money for her to go to a local college, she hires her old classmate Calvin to act as her stalker to convince to her parents to let her leave the state for Caltech.
Identifiers: LCCN 2016012541 (print) | LCCN 2016017457 (ebook) | ISBN 9781462118670 (pbk.) | ISBN 9781462126521
Subjects: | CYAC: Honesty--Fiction. | Stalkers--Fiction. | Maturation (Psychology)--Fiction. | College choice--Fiction. | Universities and colleges--Fiction. | LCGFT: Romance fiction.
Classification: LCC PZ7.1.K365 Ac 2016 (print) | LCC PZ7.1.K365 (ebook) | DDC
[Fic]--dc23
LC record available at https://lccn.loc.gov/2016012541

Cover design by Michelle May Ledezma
Cover design © 2016 by Cedar Fort, Inc.
Edited and typeset by Justin Greer

Printed in the United States of America

10 9 8 7 6 5 4 3 2 1

Printed on acid-free paper

To my sisters, whose beauty and brilliance are no accident.

Chapter 1

I have a stalker."

Everyone in the kitchen turns and looks at me, almost in unison. Even The Noise is quiet, which is a miracle, considering it's nearly feeding time.

A wicked streak of energy fires through my body. I have hooked them. Suddenly nothing matters more than convincing my family that what I have just said is true.

"Today I had the star shell tortoise out at work," I say. "You know, for the kids to come up and pet. This really skeezy guy just watched me the whole time. Right as I was putting the tortoise back in its cage, he stroked my arm and asked me if he was allowed to touch all the animals at the zoo."

Despite herself, my sister Heather looks genuinely interested in what I'm saying. Usually she either mocks me or ignores me altogether. This behavior is not without cause. She still hasn't forgiven me for taking her place as the baby in the family.

"Ew, Sabrina, that's just gross." Heather shifts The Noise in her arms, and the baby's little chubby legs press deeper into her stomach. She still has a jelly belly from her pregnancy, even though she faithfully belts The Noise and Mack into a double jogging stroller and runs three miles every morning. I place my hands on my hips and nod emphatically.

"It's pretty creepy," I say, adjusting my safari hat. I have landed a summer job as an Adventure Pal at the zoo and the safari hat is part of my uniform. It's completely unnecessary to wear it here, at home, but I wear it anyway. I like to think it grants me an aura of authority.

Dad is standing at the kitchen island, sorting through the mail. His hand hovers over the free Costco magazine, which features a graying man with glasses and the headline "Costco Members Defy Stereotype." He sweeps the magazine across the counter toward the rest of the junk mail and then looks squarely at me.

"Sounds kind of serious, Sabby-apple."

Dad's response is, of course, predictable. Mom's is not. Even though she is up to her elbows in a tossed salad, she stills her hands long enough to smother me with a look that nearly qualifies as concerned. Then her eyes flit to the kitchen timer and she motions to the dining area. For Mom, no crisis can compete with the urgency of hot rolls in the oven.

"Sabrina," Mom says, "set the table."

"Heather's not doing anything," I say.

"Your sister is taking care of her children." As if to prove this point, Heather presses the baby deeper into her flabby stomach and heads toward Mack, who is quietly pushing a Matchbox car across the floor. Other than the fact that he is naked from the waist up, Mack hardly looks like he needs taking care of. But it doesn't matter. Heather never sets the table, even when she doesn't have an excuse not to.

I brush past Heather and fire off a dirty look. I still haven't forgiven her for moving back home. In fact, I tried to punish her by plastering a bumper sticker on my Corolla that says "Drive Carefully—90% of People Are Caused by Accidents." Of course, she just laughed when she saw it, because Mack and The Noise aren't the only accidents running around our house. There's a reason Heather and I are ten years apart. I'm an accident too.

This is why I set the table, even though I don't want to. This is why I never do anything wrong. I mean, I've made mistakes, obviously, but basically I've always done what's expected of me. I've never even done anything kind of bad, like toilet papered the neighbor's house or sneaked into a movie theater or kissed a boy. I just graduated from Skyview High with a perfect 4.0 grade point average. When you're born an accident, you have something to prove.

Only doing the right thing doesn't get you any attention at all. When Heather announced she was pregnant with The Noise, Dad came home from work early and, after a tear-fest, we all went out to dinner at the Olive Garden. When I announced I had been accepted to Caltech, Mom gave me a weak sideways hug and then asked me to take out the garbage.

I'm like all the essays I turned in for AP English—black and white and plain all over. No lovely slashes of red ink to spice me up. Until now. I can feel the scales of attention tipping toward me, and, to keep the momentum going, I elaborate on the whole stalker thing.

"This isn't just some isolated event," I say as I open the utensil drawer and count out four pewter knives. "Security had a girl in admin look this guy up. Turns out, he's a member. So she pulled up his membership history. Last year, he came to the zoo a total of eight times. Since I started work last month, he's already been seventeen times."

Dad quits sorting the mail. He looks genuinely worried. I have a nagging feeling that I should stop. Dad may be the only person in the whole world who really loves me and this stalker thing might seriously upset him. He's about to say something, but then a neon yellow postcard on the counter catches his eye. I notice it just a half second after he does, and, when I see it, the nagging feeling returns.

Dad holds up the postcard and wags it in front of me. "Why would Caltech be sending you a notice about orientation?"

I resist the urge to rip the card from his hand, and as casually as I can, I walk toward him and pretend to take a better look.

"That's strange," I say. "It must have been sent in error."

"See?" Dad says. "Just another reason not to go to that crummy school."

Caltech has the best biology program in the country. It is anything but a crummy school. But Dad knows that. After how much I've talked about Caltech this past year, everyone in my family knows that. But, despite the caliber of their bio department, my parents have decided I will attend Boise State in the fall. Mom says she wants me to go to Boise State because it's close to home, but she really wants me to go there because it's affordable. Dad says he wants me to go to Boise State because it's affordable, but he really wants me to go there because it's close to home. Close to him. He worries about me.

I say I am going to Boise State because it's expected of me. But I'm not going. You know that whole "I've never done anything wrong" shtick? It's not entirely true. There is one thing I've done wrong. This spring, after I received the acceptance letter from Caltech, I returned the enclosed postcard with a nice, black check mark in the box labeled "Attend."

Only now, with concern practically oozing from Dad's eyeballs, I almost decide to confess the whole thing. But then The Noise starts crying again, that kind of jarring, high-pitched wailing that really does a number on my nerves. I want to go to Caltech. I hear the crying, I see the neon yellow postcard, and suddenly, something dawns on me. My stalker may do more for me than just earn me a little attention. He may just be my ticket out of here.

This is why I look straight at Dad when I deliver the last zinger of the evening. Because if I need to play to anyone's sympathy, it's his.

"Security said I should watch, just to make sure this guy doesn't start following me home. If he does, they said I should look into getting a restraining order."

The color drains right out of Dad's face. Bull's-eye.

Maybe, just maybe, if I can convince Dad that I'm in enough danger at home, he won't mind shipping me to California for school. But there's only one problem. If I hope to pull this stalker scheme off, I'm going to need more than just a scary story.

Chapter 2

I desperately need to find a stalker.

As soon as dinner is over, everyone migrates to the adjoining family room. It's Monday, which means *The Bachelorette* is on. Mom and Heather settle into the couch and launch into a lively debate about which contestant is going home tonight. Dad sets *Candy Land* up on the coffee table for Mack while bouncing The Noise on his knee. I stay put in the kitchen and whip out my phone. For the moment at least, I am guaranteed some uninterrupted screen time.

Desperate times call for desperate measures. And so, I turn to the only source I can think of for advice: Cleverbot.

I type: *I desperately need to find a stalker.*

The blue cursor blinks back at me. Seconds pass. I think, for a moment, that I have stumped it. Cleverbot can only respond to my question with a phrase from its massive database of previous conversations. Surely, no one has made this statement to Cleverbot before. But then the blinking cursor is replaced by a line of text, text that is strikingly on point: *So you admit to being a liar.*

You got me, Cleverbot. I lied. But it's not like I intended to. The lie wasn't premeditated. In fact, there is a kernel of truth to this whole stalker story. Okay, maybe not a kernel, but a grain. A speck of truth. Today, as I was putting the tortoise back in its cage, I noticed that a cute guy was watching me. Okay, looking at me. A cute guy at the zoo looked at me. That's kind of the same thing as being stalked, isn't it?

I fire back at Cleverbot with: *I didn't mean to lie, it just slipped out.*

—*It's okay. I understand.*

—*At least you do. I don't think my parents will be as forgiving.*

—*One never stops learning.*

Oh Cleverbot, is there no end to your wisdom?

Call it force of habit, but I end the conversation with the same question I always end our conversations with.

—*Cleverbot, will you marry me?*

—*Of course!*

The theme song for *The Bachelorette* begins and Mom and Heather stop chatting. This season's bachelorette just happens to be Jordan Greene, a girl who went to high school with Heather. Jordan Greene is generically beautiful—blonde, thin, symmetrical. Heather is convinced that Jordan's had plastic surgery, although she can find nothing in the tabloids that confirms this suspicion. There have, however, been plenty of stories linking Jordan romantically to Heather's ex-boyfriend, Thayne Stockett, but Heather has dismissed these claims as flat-out lies. It may be the only thing Heather's read in a celebrity magazine that she hasn't embraced as truth.

Heather acts like Jordan is ridiculous for being on the show, but I can tell she's totally jealous. Every time the show features Jordan in a bikini (which is practically every episode), Heather says, "Look at her abs!" and then looks at her own jiggly stomach in disgust.

I have endured more than my fair share of awful TV since Heather moved back home. Before *The Bachelorette* there was *Real Housewives* and *Jersey Shore*. The only thing she's watched that hasn't made me want to vomit is *Jurassic Park*. This was during Mack's dinosaur phase and Heather, with her characteristic bad judgment, thought it would be a great movie to show a five-year-old. It was your classic train wreck. Poor Mack had nightmares for weeks after, even though, at the time, he watched the whole thing, his eyes practically superglued to the screen. I couldn't look away from the screen either. This is because I still haven't outgrown my dinosaur phase. This is also because I am kind of in love with Jeff Goldblum. His tall, dark handsomeness has a wonderful twist of geek that I find irresistible.

At the commercial break Heather pulls herself off the couch and wanders back into the kitchen. I instinctively shield my phone as she walks past the table, even though her eyes are glued to her own. She manipulates the screen with one hand and grabs a glass from the cupboard with the other. Heather leans into the counter, absently filling the glass with tap water, when, without warning, she squeals.

"Paul Nelson just messaged me on Facebook. He wants to take me to dinner tomorrow!" None of us respond. She shuts off the faucet, leaving the glass in the sink. "Anyone up for watching the kids for me?"

"I'm showing houses tomorrow night," Mom calls from the couch. Mom's a real estate agent, or, as she likes to say, a "real-a-tour." She says it like selling houses is something exotic, and not just an excuse to wear Ann Taylor separates and put her cheesy picture on business cards.

Heather turns to look at Dad so fast I think her neck might snap. "Dad?"

Dad sighs and then nods without much enthusiasm. No one is too excited about Heather dating again. She doesn't have a very good track record.

Heather returns to the couch with a noticeable spring in her step. I return to my phone, equally elated. Heather has unwittingly given me some direction in my stalker search. I abandon my beloved Cleverbot for vile Facebook, where I am instantly assaulted by the News Feed. Heather (of course) is "Going on a date!" Michelle (from work) is "Making Chicken ala King for dinner." Tyler (my oldest and only brother) is "Having a case of the Mondays." I click on *Like* and watch as a small thumbs up sign appears with the text "Sabrina Likes This." Really, I don't. Tyler is always having a case of the Mondays. At least, I think he is. I don't really know Tyler, seeing as how he's thirteen years older than me and moved out when I was six years old. He lives in Milwaukee and does marketing for Kohl's. Mom keeps his bedroom for him for when he comes to visit at Christmas. His room is exactly how he left it—down to the posters of Smashing Pumpkins and Stone Temple Pilots tacked to the wall and the lingering odor of adolescence.

I pull myself away from the News Feed and tab over to my profile. My wall boasts a picture of me holding Snowy, the zoo's barn owl, with the caption "Lord of the Wings." Michelle from work "likes this." I am tempted to view

Michelle's wall, but then I glance at the TV and see the host, Chris Harrison, a line of generically handsome guys in suits, and Jordan Greene, who, at the moment, is looking a little bit stressed. This spectacle can only mean one thing: the rose ceremony. This dreadful show is almost over, and I'm about to lose my moment of solitude.

I scan the pictures of my friends on the sidebar. I am looking for someone who could possibly pass as "skeezy." Also, someone my family doesn't know. And, perhaps most important, someone male. Finding a friend who fits these criteria is difficult, because my use of Facebook is governed by one simple principle—I am only virtual friends with people I am actual friends with in real life. This is why I only have like thirty-seven Facebook friends. Curse my principles. I need a bigger pool.

I pass over pictures of Heather and Tyler and Michelle. Ella Anderson, the closest thing I had to a best friend at Skyview High, will have to do. I tap her profile picture and scan her wall. Her last status update announces that she is "Going dark." She left the day after graduation for some remote village in Guatemala, where she plans to spend the summer building schoolhouses—never mind the fact she's never hefted a hammer.

I check out her friends and scroll through what must be Skyview's entire student body. Ella is nothing if not thorough. She's even friends with Aunt Ilene, the lunch lady. I view face after smiling face, and then I find him. Calvin. We had precalculus together my sophomore year. He sat in the back row, behind the girl who popped her whiteheads in class. He was a senior and by far the smartest guy in the room, even though he had failed the class the first time. Calvin is one of those guys who is too smart for his own good.

I check out his wall. Most of his pictures are of himself. At least we have that in common. He is president of the Game Club at Boise State, and under *Activities* he has an exhaustive list of what must be every board game in existence, along with a rating on a 1–10 scale. Under *Interests* he has listed, simply, "Bears." He is so weird.

I click back on his profile pic and assess for a minute. He hasn't changed much since high school—except now he has kind of a Zach Galifianakis beard thing going. He is still rail thin and has wild, dark hair and huge eyes. I can tell all this even though, in his profile pic, half of his face is hidden behind a ping-pong paddle. I study his picture again. Yeah, this guy could definitely pass as a stalker.

I tap the *Add Friend* button and take a beat. In the living room, The Noise is crying and Jordan Greene is holding out a wilted rose to a cardboard cutout posing as a human person. Despite the wailing and the TV volume I still manage to hear my phone ping. Calvin has not only accepted my friend request, he's also sent me a message. Granted, the entirety of said message is *Howdy*, but it's an opening all the same. My heart does a nosedive for my stomach. It is now or never.

—*I have a proposition for you.*
—*Interesting . . .*
—*It's strictly business.*
—*Deets?*

Details. He wants details. I am about to type something like *I want to pay you to stalk me,* but I can't. It's just too ridiculous.

—*Let's discuss in person. What's your tomorrow like?*

—*Like the Grand Canyon.*

— *?*

—*It's wide open.*

I look at his dorky profile pic and smirk. Of course it is.

Chapter 3

The next morning I head for the Starbucks near the zoo where I have arranged to meet Calvin. I arrive promptly at ten o'clock. The café is quiet. I adjust my safari hat and scout the place out. Besides the two sullen baristas behind the counter, the only other person I see is a middle-aged man wearing a T-shirt that says "Conserve water, drink beer." He is plowing into a muffin and washing it down with a giant cup of coffee. So much for conservation.

I can't believe I am about to ask a guy to pretend-stalk me. My whole body feels shaky. Obviously, I'm out of my element here. I try channeling my inner-Heather and pretend that I can act without worrying about the consequences. When that doesn't work, I just focus on Caltech. Caltech, Caltech, Caltech.

I wander toward the window and look for Calvin. Maybe I have missed him. Or, more realistically, maybe he just isn't coming at all. I mean, when has a guy shown up for me, ever?

If I were Heather, he would be here. Even with her post-pregnancy ab flab, she still can turn heads. But then, Heather has never had a problem getting attention from guys. Hot ones too. Thayne Stockett, Baby Daddy #1, was the state wrestling champion in high school and is now a semi-professional Ultimate Fighter. Baby Daddy #2 played football at Boise State and is now a personal trainer at Gold's Gym.

I glance at my watch. 10:15. He's not coming. I can't help feeling a little disappointed. I mean, I'm no Heather, but Calvin's no Baby Daddy either.

I have some time to kill before my shift at the zoo, so I decide to get something to eat. I gaze up at the menu and one of the baristas steps up to the counter, looking expectantly at me. I'm just about to order when I hear a sharp hiss from across the room.

"Do you know that guy?" the barista asks.

I turn behind me, but the only person I see is the middle-aged man in the lame T-shirt.

"What guy?"

"That guy," she says, pointing toward a huge potted plant in the corner of the café.

I look again, and there, hidden behind the bright green leaves of the plant, is Calvin. He is wearing those plastic glasses that are attached to a huge nose and a black moustache. When he sees me, he waves.

"Oh, that guy," I say. "We're just Facebook friends." I can feel myself blush. If I had to rank my embarrassment on the salsa scale, it would have just ricocheted to hot. Muy caliente. I turn from the counter and walk toward the big potted plant and the master of disguise.

"Hi, Calvin." Just for the record, his real name isn't Calvin. It's Brad Klein. In high school, everyone called him Calvin, because of the underwear, and the nickname stuck.

"What's with the disguise?"

"What's with yours?" He gives me a good once-over. I am dressed in hiking boots, khaki shorts, a black polo shirt, and, of course, my safari hat.

"This," I say, rather grandly, "is my uniform. I'm an Adventure Pal at the zoo."

Calvin unfolds himself from behind the plant and looms over me. My goodness, he's tall. Like, Jeff Goldblum tall—who is 6'4" in stockinged feet. I place a hand on the table beside me to steady myself and angle my head back to meet his gaze.

"What took you so long to find me?"

"I didn't realize I had invited you here to play a game of hide and seek." I break eye contact with him and take a seat at the table. "Besides, I wasn't looking for Groucho Marx."

Calvin takes a seat next to me. He smiles broadly and then takes off his dumb disguise and stashes it in his messenger bag. "Well, I wasn't looking for Pippi Longstocking, but I had no problem spotting you." He reaches across the table and tugs on one of my braids. I swat his hand away and then take off my safari hat and fluff my bangs with my fingers. I pretend not to notice that my hands are trembling.

In my mind, I have already rehearsed how this meeting will go down. I'll start with some small talk, then segue into detailing how going to Caltech is my heart's desire, and then, reasonably, explain how having a fake stalker is the only way to get there. But Calvin is zeroing in on me with his huge eyes and everything inside of me kind of gets flipped around. I don't remember where to begin. I also don't remember Calvin's eyes being so startlingly blue.

"I want to pay you to stalk me," I blurt out.

Impossibly, Calvin's big, blue eyes get even bigger. "Wow," he says, stroking his beard. "That was . . . unexpected."

"Well, yeah." Inside I am reeling. Unexpected is not my territory. "Here's the thing. I've been accepted to go to Caltech in the fall. But my parents—well, really, my dad—is worried about me being so far away from home. I'm thinking, if I can convince him that I'm in some sort of danger here, California will almost look like—"

"Refuge." Calvin turns from me and looks vacantly at the ground for a minute. There is something about this guy that makes me uncomfortable. Finally, he returns his attention to me. "So, what exactly are you proposing?"

"Nothing too invasive," I say, trying to smile. "I was thinking maybe you could just kind of, you know, drive past my house a few times—just enough to scare my dad a little."

"Isn't there an easier way to go about this?"

"Like what?"

"Like, forget all the stagecraft and just go to Caltech."

"But my parents don't want me to go." It seems like a perfectly valid counterargument, but Calvin looks unconvinced. Obviously, he doesn't lead a life that requires perfection. I can feel Caltech slipping through my fingers. "Look, if you do this for me, I'll pay you fifty bucks."

If I were making this offer to any other guy, he would stand up and walk away. But Calvin isn't any other guy.

"I could stand to make some coin," he says. "I'm not exactly working at the moment."

"Big school load?"

"Nah. But, you know, jobs are so . . . rigid. I don't like to get involved with anything that limits me." He focuses on me again with those huge eyes and then kind of half smiles. "If I do this, you're going to go all *Pretty Woman* on me, aren't you, Sabrina?"

"What?"

"You know, like that old Julia Roberts movie where the guy falls head over heels for this . . ."

"I know the movie." I've never seen it, but I'm familiar enough with the plot. Does he really think I'm going to fall in love with him? Sorry, Calvin. Not. A. Chance.

"Well?" he asks.

"No, I'm not going to go all *Pretty Woman* on you."

"Good." He glances down at the table, almost like he's disappointed. But then he flashes me that big smile of his and claps his hands together. "Well, in that case, I'm in."

Despite his intolerance for limits, Calvin and I hash out the details of our plan. After a few rounds of negotiating, we agree that the fifty-dollar payment will buy me five drive-bys from Calvin. Ten bucks a pop seems a little steep to me, but if it gets me to Caltech in the end, it will be money well spent. We exchange phone numbers and, of course, I give Calvin directions to my house on Greenwood Drive. Things go pretty smoothly, until one of the baristas decides to take a smoke break. As soon as she steps outside, Calvin keeps a steady gaze on the lone barista at the counter. The moment she steps through the swinging doors into the stock room, Calvin clutches his messenger bag to his chest and stands up.

"Meet me outside," he says.

"What?"

"Outside," he says, raising his eyebrows for emphasis. Calvin darts toward the cash register and, in one deft movement, removes the tip jar from the counter, dumps the contents into his messenger bag, and then ducks out the door.

I dumbly follow him outside, stunned. Calvin is already halfway down the block, resting against a rusted red Ford Escort. I march towards him, trying to shake the feeling that I have just aided and abetted a criminal.

"What was that?" I ask.

"Opportunity."

"That's funny. Most people would call it stealing."

"You and I," he says, flashing me a conspiratorial smile, "are not most people."

"I wouldn't do something like that."

"Wouldn't you?" He steps away from the car and kind of towers over me for a minute, making me feel incredibly inconsequential. I look away from Calvin and study the Ford Escort instead. The rear window is all but consumed by a sticker of the comic strip Calvin urinating on a Ford logo. The image is surprising enough that I forget my righteous indignation and look at Calvin again.

"Is this your car?"

Calvin nods.

"It's a Ford, you know." I look at the sticker again and

smile. The car is practically rotting away, but the Calvin sticker makes it especially conspicuous. Oh, Dad is going to notice this.

"Are we still on for tonight?" Calvin asks, sidestepping an explanation of the stupid sticker.

I try to forget the incident with the tip jar and take a deep breath. "Sure."

"Cool beans." Calvin reaches toward me and tugs one of my braids again. This time, I don't bother to swat his hand away. Instead, I stand motionless on the sidewalk and watch him leave. As his car hurtles out of sight, my stomach stops functioning as an organ and pretends it's an acrobat. I'm not surprised. After all, I just gave Mr. Limitless my address.

Chapter 4

After work I race home and wait to be stalked. I keep bouncing into the front room to peer out the window, searching for Calvin's rusted red Ford Escort. I am completely unnerved, but luckily for me, no one notices. Mom, of course, is off showing houses, and Dad is out picking up dinner from Little Caesars. Heather is running around like a banshee, preparing for her impending date, and, in the process, completely neglecting Mack and The Noise.

I plop down on the couch and scan my phone, trying to collect my thoughts. BuzzFeed is featuring a story with the headline "Soccer Player Injured by Bobblehead." The story strikes me as terribly unnecessary. I don't need to be reminded that great big empty heads can really do some damage.

The Noise crawls over and petitions for my attention with his chubby little hands, but I can't be bothered. I am trying to get my own bobblehead to solve the problem of how to get Dad to notice Calvin and his Ford Escort. I thought the biggest obstacle in this whole scheme would be finding a stalker. But now, I can't get my mind to jump over the hurdle of ensuring that Dad actually sees him. And so, of course, I consult Cleverbot.

I pull up the app and type: *How will I get Dad to notice Calvin?*

Cleverbot responds with: *Which wedding?*

Fantastic. Just one empty bobblehead talking to another.

I am still working on a game plan when Dad arrives with a pizza and a greasy bag of Crazy Bread. "Soup's on!" he says, slapping the cardboard box on the counter. Mack scrambles to the kitchen with The Noise right at his heels. Dad scoops the baby up in his arms and quiets him with a breadstick. Leave it to Dad to restore things to order. I wander into the kitchen, plunge my hand into the bag of Crazy Bread, and fish out a breadstick. I gnaw on it for a minute, waiting for Dad to ask about my day so I can tell another whopper about my stalker. But before he gives me his attention, Heather bursts into the kitchen and steals it for herself.

"Heather," Dad says, beaming at her. "Don't you look nice."

Dad couldn't have chosen a more underwhelming adjective. Heather doesn't look nice—she looks like she's auditioning for president of the PTA. She must have raided Mom's closet, because as far as I'm aware, her wardrobe doesn't include clothing that could be described as respectable. She looks all prim and proper and Pollyanna-ish. Something is up.

Dad walks over to Heather and plants a kiss on top of her head. Heather doesn't know how good she has it. All she has to do to earn Dad's approval is throw on a pair of mom jeans.

"My date should be here soon," she says, glancing at her watch.

"Remind me who you're going out with again," Dad says.

"Paul Nelson." The Noise reaches for her, but Heather takes one look at his parmesan-smeared face and steps away.

"Tell me why that name sounds so familiar," Dad says, shifting the baby in his arms.

"Dad," Heather says, "he's our dentist." She blushes. "He asked me out at my last checkup."

Inwardly, I groan. The whole arrangement seems a little disgusting to me. It's not like Paul Nelson is ancient or any-thing—he just took over Dr. Allen's practice last year. But the idea of going out with a guy who knows the location of every filling in your mouth disturbs me. I raise an eye-brow in Dad's direction, but instead of looking upset by this bomb, he seems genuinely pleased.

"Paul Nelson." Dad pats Heather on the back. I'm sur-prised he doesn't offer to give her a high five. I guess I can't really blame him. After all, unlike Heather's other boy-friends, Paul Nelson could easily afford to pay child support.

High on the good news, Dad forgets the pizza and me altogether and escorts Heather into the front room to wait for Paul. I follow quietly behind them, making sure that Dad sits on the sofa facing the window. At least now Dad has a chance of spotting Calvin. I cast nervous glances out the window and Heather looks repeatedly at her watch. Paul is late. Heather doesn't say anything, but I can tell she's worried he won't show. I know the feeling.

My cell phone beeps. I have a text from Calvin. *Be there in 5*. Heather and Dad are both looking intently out the window and Calvin is on his way. I couldn't have planned this better if I'd tried. As long as Paul doesn't show up in the next few minutes, Dad is certain to see old rusty.

Minutes pass. Dad suggests that Heather give Paul a call, but Heather just shrugs. Her curled hair starts to look deflated. I gaze helplessly at the empty street. Where is Calvin?

"He's here!" Mack says, pressing his face to the window.

A shiny black Lexus rolls up to the curb. Heather hops up and runs to the door. "Don't embarrass me," she hisses at Dad, just before she swings the door open and flashes a toothy smile in Paul's direction. I check Paul out as he walks up to the house. I don't know what Heather's worried about. I mean, the guy is wearing a braided leather belt. And he's balding. Heather is going out with a guy who is balding. Now I've seen everything.

Heather reluctantly brings Paul into the front room for introductions. Dad gives him a hearty handshake and Paul makes a fuss over Heather's kids. I can tell Heather's dying for the niceties to end, but I do my best to prolong them. I need to keep Dad in this room until Calvin drives by.

When Paul asks how I'm doing, I launch into a detailed description of my duties at the zoo, keeping one eye on Paul and the other on the window. Paul humors me with his attention, but Heather has heard this spiel one too many times.

"Sabrina," she says, cutting me off mid-sentence by placing a firm hand on my arm. "Paul made dinner reservations." She places extra emphasis on "reservations," as if it's the most chivalrous thing any guy's ever done for her.

"We really should get going," Paul says. He gives Heather a stupid, gooey look and she nearly melts right there on the carpet. Ugh. I rack my brain, but I can't think of anything to say that's going to draw Paul away from Heather now. He places his hand on the small of her back, and, despite The Noise's cries in protest and my own silent pleading, he ushers Heather out the front door.

The instant they're gone, Mack starts whining for a drink, and before I can stop him, Dad rushes into the kitchen to get one. I can guess what's going to happen next, but I look out the window anyway. Sure enough, the moment Dad leaves the front room, a rusted Ford Escort putters down the street.

· · · · · · ·

Calvin drives past the house again on Wednesday and Thursday, but of course, Dad doesn't see him these times either. Things are not going according to plan. I console myself by engaging in long, absurd conversations with Cleverbot, and then torment myself by taking virtual tours of Caltech's campus. Even online, Caltech's campus takes my breath away. Perfect, pristine buildings sit atop perfect, pristine lawns. Everything is lush and green and alive. In my estimation, Pasadena is paradise.

I check the calendar on Caltech's website and am startled to discover that classes start in just eight weeks. I am running out of time. To make things worse, on Thursday I receive an email from Caltech's housing department, reminding me that to secure a dorm room, I need to pay a fee of $2,500 by July 18th. July 18th is four weeks away. It sounds like your typical story problem: *If Sabrina needs $2,500 to get to Caltech, and she currently works twenty hours a week at a rate of $10 per hour . . .*

I leave off the mental calculations. I don't care for this particular story's ending.

I feel like the earth has swallowed me whole, but nobody in my family notices, because ever since Heather's date with Mr. Braided Leather Belt, they have taken up residence on cloud nine. It didn't help that Paul sent Heather a dozen red roses the morning after their date. I try to regain some attention by making references to my stalker, but the concept of a stalker seems less threatening once Heather and Mom do some stalking of their own and drive uptown to check out Paul's McMansion. Mom has practically planned the wedding already, and Dad, who once complained about the way Paul filled a cavity, can't stop raving about what an exceptional dentist he is.

Heather may have fooled Mom and Dad, but I personally don't see a wedding in the near future. Paul is not Heather's type. And I'm absolutely positive that Heather's interest in Paul is only as deep as his bank account.

So late Thursday night, I'm not surprised when Heather flips the TV on to Fuel. This channel is home to the Ultimate Fighting Championship league, and it's obvious that Heather is looking for Thayne Stockett, better known as Baby Daddy #1. Heather's never recovered from their breakup, and she torments herself by watching this barbarism late at night, the same way I torment myself by taking virtual tours of Caltech's campus.

I join Heather on the couch. Misery does love her some company. Only tonight, Heather doesn't seem that miserable. In fact, just seconds after the camera pans over Thayne and his hot muscle-bound body, Heather changes the channel to TLC.

"You're going to miss the fight," I say over the opening credits of *What Not to Wear*.

She shrugs, and then looks absently at me for a minute. Heather is definitely lost in thought. I hope she's not thinking about Paul. Nothing good will come of that relationship.

"You know," I say, "statistically, dentists have the highest suicide rate of any profession."

It's a rotten thing to say, but I figure someone in this family needs to talk some sense into her. When Heather turns to look at me, presumably to come back with some verbal barb of her own, her auburn hair falls softly around her face. Even in the synthetic blue glow of the television, she still looks pretty. For once, I don't envy her beauty. She may have the looks, but I have the brains. And I'm smart enough not to fall for the wrong guy.

Chapter 5

I spend the better part of my Friday morning in the zoo's small animal house with Lonestar, the nine-banded armadillo. The building is hot, cramped, and smells worse than a boys' locker room, but I can't complain because Lonestar is one of my favorite animals to handle. He is delightfully odd. The kids think so too, as evidenced by their squeals of astonishment as they crowd around me, eager to take a turn to pet his armored shell.

"Two fingers," I yell over the kids' heads, holding up my index and middle fingers to demonstrate the way they can touch Lonestar. For the most part, the children comply with this direction and restrain their mauling of Lonestar to two-fingered pokes and prods. While Lonestar patiently endures these weakened attacks, I deliver my talking points to anyone within earshot. I say that armadillo is a Spanish word meaning "little armored one," and that armadillos are closely related to anteaters and sloths. When I say that armadillos' unlucky propensity for being run over by cars has earned them the nickname "hillbilly speed bumps," everyone, even the adults, laughs. This is another reason why I love my job: I am guaranteed a captive audience.

Of course, it's not really me they're captivated by. It's

Lonestar. I try not to brood on this distinction and pretend that the crowd around me has formed, in part, because of my animated talking points. But really, a corpse could manage to draw a crowd here, as long as it had a live animal in hand.

When it's time for my break I head over to the Oasis for a Coke. Last night I stayed up too late watching TV with Heather, and I am paying for it now. I collapse onto a bench, take off my safari hat, and shake out my hair, which is still damp from my morning shower. I drape my hair over the bench and turn my face to the sun and enjoy a moment of pure relaxation. The moment is brief. The zoo is busy, even for a Friday, and the ensuing noise interrupts my attempt at Zen. Begrudgingly, I sit up straight and people-watch, an activity that is, at first, amusing, and then slightly terrifying. Because when I start to break the mass of people down into parts, it dawns on me that none of them are alone. There are moms pushing strollers and seniors clutching sturdy arms and couples holding hands. Everyone has someone. Someone to talk to or laugh with or cling to.

Everyone except me.

In desperation, I put my safari hat back on. I have the horrible suspicion that I am about to cry. And then, wonderfully, someone looks at me. This someone not only looks at me, he smiles.

"Calvin," I say. He ambles over toward me and sits beside me on the bench. I don't know what has me more surprised—that Calvin is here, or that his knee is touching mine. I look into his big, blue eyes with something not unlike wonder.

"What are you doing here?"

He leans in so close to me that I can feel the stray ends of his beard against my cheek.

"I'm stalking you." His voice is almost a whisper. The rational part of me realizes that this is kind of a creepy thing to say. The rational part of me realizes that getting involved with the guy I'm paying to stalk me is even more disturbing than going out with my dentist.

"You're doing a pretty good job," I whisper back.

The rational part of me has left the building.

"Am I?" Calvin repositions himself on the bench, ostensibly to get a better look at me, and as a result, his knee no longer touches mine. Maybe it's this sudden loss of physical contact, maybe it's the caffeine kicking in, but thankfully, I come to my senses. Calvin is not doing a pretty good job of stalking me. Actually, he is doing a terrible job. Despite the way he is—dare I say?—drinking me in with his eyes, I refuse to swoon.

"Really, Calvin, what are you doing here?"

"I wanted to see you." He kind of crooks his head to one side and looks me over again. "Although, you looked a lot better without the hat."

"How long have you been watching me?" I instinctively grab the brim of my hat and give it a good solid tug downward.

"Long enough."

An awkward silence follows this rather cryptic remark. *Long enough for what?* I wonder. Calvin makes no attempt to clarify this for me. Instead he just continues to look at me in a way that girls like me aren't supposed to be looked at. I am more than a little uncomfortable.

"Don't you have, like, something to do during the day?" I try to maintain control of my heart, which has suddenly decided it wants to run away from me.

Calvin gives a nonchalant little shrug and points to the drink in my hand.

"What's your poison?" he asks.

"What?"

"What are you drinking?"

"Coke."

Without asking, he takes the cup from my hand, and in the process his fingers brush against mine. He removes the lid and takes a swig of the soda, and then rests the cup possessively on his knee, like it's been his all along.

"So," he says, chewing on a piece of ice, "is Daddy scared yet?"

"No."

"Because?"

"Because, Kleinstein, he hasn't actually seen you yet." My pretend stalker is so close I can touch him, but Caltech has never felt farther away. I am seriously beginning to wonder if my exit strategy is going to work. Even if Dad catches a glimpse of Calvin in his rusted Ford Escort, so what? Is that really going to be enough of a threat to convince him that I need to flee the state?

I turn from Calvin and stare hard at the glimmering black pavement.

"Let's not prolong this," I finally say. "You can stop stalking me now. My parents are never going to let me go to Caltech."

"Why is it so important for you to go to Caltech, anyway?"

"Because it has one of the best biology programs in the country, but it's not Stanford or Harvard."

"So going there wouldn't be a cliché," he says.

"Exactly." No one has ever understood this before. Almost intuitively, I take off my safari hat and stash it in my lap. I kind of fan my hair out over my shoulders and give Calvin my best attempt at a dazzling smile. "Caltech is like the MIT of the West," I continue. "Its enrollment is small—like less than a thousand undergrads—and they do research for places like NASA. Plus, it's in Southern California." I sigh. "But come fall, I'll still be here, where my parents want me, attending Boise State."

"Hey," Calvin says, "Boise State's not that bad."

"I know." I've heard the sales pitch from Mom at least a hundred times. "It's just, the only thing Boise State's known for is football."

"And Caltech?"

"Caltech doesn't even have a team." I smile victoriously. "Look, I'm sure, like my mom says, I could get a 'quality' education at Boise State. It's just, you know, that's where half of the kids from Skyview end up. Going there would be like high school all over again, but on a bigger scale."

"Poor Sabrina." Calvin pulls his face into a mock frown. "Were the kids mean to you in school?"

"No." Despite myself, I cross my arms tightly against my chest. Calvin may be teasing, but he's still hit a nerve. "They weren't mean to me. They just didn't notice me."

"And you want to go to a place where you'll feel special?"

"I want to go to a place where I'll fit in."

Our eyes lock. I get the sense that Calvin knows where I'm coming from.

"Sabrina, you can just go to Caltech, you know. You're an adult. You don't need your parents' permission."

I may not technically need my parents' permission to go to Caltech, but I most certainly need their blessing.

"You don't understand my family," I say.

"What don't I understand?" He scoots closer to me until his thigh is pressed against mine. Maybe it's the sudden rush of physical contact, maybe it's the way that Calvin has just rescued me from drowning in a sea of anonymity, but, curiously, I start talking. I tell Calvin about Dad, who is basically wonderful despite a lackluster career as a claims examiner at the Idaho Farm Bureau. I tell him about Mom and her cheesy business cards and the obnoxious way she pronounces realtor. She's always been preoccupied with money, I say, but now that she and Dad are nearing retirement, she is especially anxious about their finances.

Money is one of the reasons she wants me to stay at home and attend Boise State, I tell Calvin, even though, when my oldest brother Tyler graduated high school, Mom nearly forced him to attend Gonzaga, although she had to go to work full-time to help pay for tuition. I tell him that Tyler dropped out of school his sophomore year anyway, and basically wasted most of his twenties working odd jobs until finally settling for a lackluster job of his own with the marketing department at Kohl's.

Then I tell Calvin about Heather, and how she moved in with Thayne Stockett after high school, despite my parents' vehement protests. I describe how I know more about Mixed Martial Arts than anyone would expect, and complain about the way I was basically forced to follow Thayne's rise from an unknown fighter in the local Boise MMA league to an almost celebrity in the UFC, and how this relative fame and fortune caused Thayne to lose interest in Heather, even after Mack was born. I talk about Heather's heartbreak, and her rebound with the Gold's Gym trainer, and about how that decision landed her back home, bringing with her Mack and The Noise and an endless array of terrible television programs.

I am completely rambling, but Calvin is hanging onto my every word, and it dawns on me: I have earned a captive audience without any assistance from beast or fowl.

"I can't figure you out, Sabrina," Calvin says when I finally stop talking.

"What don't you get?"

"You won't go to Caltech without your parents' approval. But from the sound of things, your siblings don't seem too concerned about disappointing your parents."

"Yeah, well, my siblings don't have to validate their existence."

"And you do?" Calvin says, raising an eyebrow.

"I'm different." The words I'm about to say are terrible, and I bite my lower lip to stop myself from crying. "I'm an accident."

"Aren't we all?"

"No! Not all of us. My parents planned on having Tyler and Heather. They didn't plan on me. Tyler and Heather can afford to make mistakes of their own. I can't."

"Sabrina, you don't have to spend the rest of your life proving to your parents that you were worth having."

I want to believe him, but I can't. Instead I turn away from him and study the pavement again. I glance at my watch and notice that my break ended nearly ten minutes ago.

"I really should get back to work."

"You can't get back to work yet. You still haven't given me the tour."

Calvin stands up and offers me his hand. I gaze up at him, which requires tipping my head back to take in all of his height. Maybe I'm completely losing my mind, but for an instant he looks like a quirky take on the whole tall, dark, and handsome thing. Like Jeff Goldblum with a beard. He is waiting for me to take his hand, and despite my better judgment, I do. It's like that scene in *Mary Poppins* where Mary takes Bert's hand and they magically step into the landscape he's drawn with chalk on the sidewalk. I take Calvin's hand and suddenly a world I once considered flat and two-dimensional transforms into a full and vibrant 3D.

We saunter over to the Primate House and Calvin places his hand on the small of my back as he ushers me in the door. I want to show him the pair of baby lemurs that were born this spring. We push our way through the crowd and stand with our noses nearly pressed to the glass to look at the baby lemurs, which are cuddled together in the corner of their cage. Normally I can't stop talking about these adorable animals, but now, standing next to Calvin, I can't think of anything to say. Everything—time, obligations, even Caltech's stellar bio program—has completely slipped my mind. When Calvin asks me a question about the baby lemurs, the most I can do is lamely point to a sign on the wall that lists the animals' birth statistics beneath the phrase "Born in Captivity."

I read the phrase again and then cast a sidelong glance at Calvin, who is standing dangerously close to me. I wonder if I've really snagged a captive audience after all. Maybe I got it wrong. Maybe I'm the one who's captivated. Because, at the moment, all I can do is stand here and wait for Calvin to touch me again.

Chapter 6

I can't stop thinking about Calvin.

For the record, I am not really trying that hard to not think about him. In fact, ever since his unexpected visit to the zoo this afternoon, my mind has basically been lost in some strange and wonderful fantasyland.

Of course, my reality at the moment is anything but wonderful. Heather is off again with Dr. Charming, and my parents are attending a community theater's production of *Seven Brides for Seven Brothers*. By default, I am on diaper duty. Thankfully, Mack went to bed without a fuss. He has a tendency to please that I find strikingly familiar.

The Noise, on the other hand, is fuss embodied. Heather blames his disposition on colic, but I think he is just protesting his incredible bad luck. After all, the poor kid's given name is Brodie.

I turn the volume up on the TV in an attempt to drown out the crying. Miraculously, Brodie calms down. After several minutes of fruitless channel surfing, I discover, to my delight, that FX is showing *The Fly*. The movie features the 1980s version of Jeff Goldblum, which is reason enough for me to watch, even if his character does transform into something pretty hideous in the end. This is the kind of movie a future biology major like me can really geek out on—I mean, the guy has to vomit digestive enzymes onto his food in order to eat. But, despite Jeff Goldblum and all the lovely pseudo-science, I watch the movie with mixed emotions. When Jeff Goldblum turns into a monstrous man-insect and is shot to death by his love interest, I can't help but shudder. The whole movie is a chilling reminder of the horrors that occur when things don't go according to plan.

Brodie is passed out in my arms, and as the credits stream down the TV screen, I gaze at his peaceful face. The kid's a lot cuter when he's not bawling. Unfortunately, he's not likely to stay quiet for long. It is already past ten. I wonder when my parents will be home. I wonder how things are going with Heather and the dentist. And then, of course, I start wondering about Calvin. I replay our afternoon at the zoo in my mind over and over again, until my arms start to tingle from holding Brodie for so long. I really don't want Brodie to wake up again, but I also don't want to have to hold him all night. I decide to risk it and try to put him to bed. But, sure enough, the second I stand up, he wakes and immediately starts to cry.

I may be heartless, but I put Brodie in his crib anyway. His cries follow me into the living room. In frustration, I sit at the computer and turn to Cleverbot for solace.

The moment the white dialogue box appears on the screen, I pound out: *The Noise. The Noise. THE NOISE!*

Cleverbot responds with: *Changing the subject, eh?*

—*You're right. I'm really thinking about Calvin.*

—*That's cool. But are you sure you're not really in the COAST GUARD?*

Honestly Cleverbot, I'm not sure of anything right now.

Around ten thirty my cell phone rings. It's just Dad, calling to say the play ran a little long, and that he and Mom should be home in the next half hour or so. He wants to know if I'm surviving (barely) and if I've heard from Heather yet (I haven't).

I wander into the front room, sink into the sofa, and stare out the window. I try to convince myself that I'm waiting for my parents or Heather to come home, but really, I'm waiting for Calvin. This is ridiculous, because I explicitly told him this afternoon not to drive past my house anymore. This is also ridiculous because, well, because Calvin doesn't exactly fit into my life plan. If he's not going to pretend-stalk me anymore, why do I still want to see him?

I don't know why. But I do.

Even though I can't stop thinking about Calvin, and even though I am essentially just sitting around and waiting for him to show up, I am beyond surprised when, a few minutes later, he sends me a text message that reads: *Caltech or bust.* I look out the window and, sure enough, his Ford Escort is parked in front of my house.

I text back: *I can C U.*

—*Can Daddy?*

—*Home alone.*

I am not prepared for what happens next. Just seconds after I push the send button, Calvin is out of the car and on the front step. He knocks lightly on the door, and I know I should get off the sofa and let him in, but I am suddenly petrified. And it's not just because my parents may very well be home any minute—it's something more, something that

I can't quite pin down in words. I may not know why I want to see Calvin, but I am completely baffled as to why he wants to see me.

Summoning something like courage, I stagger to the entryway and open the front door. Without hesitation, Calvin steps inside and wanders into the front room. I follow him, trying my best to act casual, like having guys over is something I do all the time, when, in fact, it's never happened. He stops to study the row of pictures hanging above the mantle, the ones of Tyler, Heather, and me in our respective graduation garb. The pictures are organized chronologically, making it easy enough to compare me to Heather. Even though I have the advantage of having been photographed in the current decade, it's not hard to tell which one of us wins the beauty contest. I imagine Calvin is thinking the same thing, because he studies Heather's picture just a little too long.

"That's my sister Heather," I say lamely.

"I figured," he says, assessing the picture again. "She's pretty."

"Yeah. A real beauty queen."

"You're jealous." Calvin playfully squeezes my shoulder and then turns me toward him. He practically consumes me with his big, blue eyes. The intensity of his gaze quickly shifts the mood from playful to serious. "You shouldn't be."

Despite myself, I swoon. It is nearly impossible not to, as we are standing toe to toe, and just looking up at Calvin makes me dizzy. You know, the whole height thing. I reach for him to steady myself, and he in turn links his arms around my waist.

My parents will be home any minute. I can't imagine how I'll explain myself if they come home and find me here, locked in Calvin's arms. My mind is made up. He absolutely has to leave right now.

My body inches closer toward him.

Calvin looks at my lips, and although I've never been kissed, I've seen enough movies to guess what's about to happen. For a half second, I close my eyes, waiting. And then . . .

Nothing.

"Is that a baby crying?" Calvin releases his hold on me and glances towards the stairs.

"That," I say, "is The Noise."

"You weren't kidding," he says, plunking down on the couch. "That kid has lungs." He stretches out his long legs and folds his arms across his chest, listening to Brodie's cries amplify. "I thought you said you were home alone."

"I'm not technically home alone. I'm stuck babysitting my nephews." I try to say this in a way that implies having to stay home on a Friday night is a major imposition. I don't want to expose the complete wasteland that is my social life. "Heather's out trying to secure a husband. And my parents had tickets to a play." I glance nervously out the window. "You should go, before they come home and want an explanation."

Calvin doesn't look like he's in any hurry to leave. In fact, instead of getting up, he reaches for the photo album on the coffee table and starts leafing through the pages. Brodie is crying at full capacity now, and for my own well-being, I need him to stop. I am feeling more than a little tense.

Calvin's not only aware of this tension, he actually seems to be enjoying it. Despite the impending arrival of my parents, he continues to flip through the photo album at a torturously slow pace. Finally, he puts the album down and stands up.

"I'll leave, Sabrina," he says, "but you have to promise me one thing."

"What's that?"

"You'll let me see you tomorrow."

"Sure," I say, relieved this is the extent of the conditional.

"Meet me at the Game Shack tomorrow night. Nine-ish."

"The Game Shack? Why?"

"I've got to close up the store."

"I thought you didn't have a job."

"I don't. I'm just doing a favor for a friend in the Game Club."

Whatever. I don't have time to ask more questions. I agree to meet him and then, finally, Calvin starts for the door. He reaches for the handle, but then pauses and turns to the stairway again, listening to Brodie.

"Try a blow dryer," he says.

"What?"

"My cousin Molly had a kid that cried all the time. She'd run a blow dryer to calm her down. That or the vacuum. Something about the white noise. It's apparently soothing."

"Thank you, baby whisperer." Believe me, around this house, the old blow dryer trick has been tried, measured, and found severely wanting. I open the door and practically shove Calvin out and then race upstairs to attempt to pacify

Brodie. Thankfully I don't have to try for long, because moments later, I hear the familiar rumble of the garage door opening. I rush to greet my parents, only too happy to pass Brodie off to more capable hands.

"The baby's still up?' Mom says. She's dressed in a pretty cream blouse and a black pencil skirt and looks like the night out has rejuvenated her. Dad, on the other hand, looks tired. He lets Mom take Brodie from me without an argument. We can hear Mom hum "Bless your Beautiful Hide" as she goes up the stairs. I give Dad a sympathetic smile. He has never been a big fan of musicals.

"Thanks for watching the kids," Dad says. "You've always been such a good girl." He gently squeezes my hand. I wish he wouldn't do that. I already feel guilty enough. Dad turns to go up to bed, but when he gets to the doorway, he stalls. There's something else he wants to say. I start to worry. Because he doesn't look tired anymore. He looks concerned.

"Sabby-apple, is that guy still hanging around you at work?"

This is when I know for sure that Dad has seen Calvin and his rusted Ford Escort. I should be elated that my plan is working. I should be praising myself for my brilliance. I should be thinking of Caltech and coastal towns and freedom.

Instead, I'm thinking about Calvin.

"No," I say. "I haven't seen him around. I think I may have overreacted to the whole thing."

"Are you sure? Because you seem like something has you kind of rattled."

"It's just Brodie. Really, Dad, I'm fine."

"So you're sure you're not being stalked?"

"I'm positive."

I can tell by the look on his face that he's not entirely convinced. I guess I can't blame him. I'm not entirely convinced myself.

Chapter 7

The Game Shack used to be a Hollywood Video, back when you still had to actually leave the house to rent a movie. A large canvas sign hangs over the entrance, announcing the arrival of this new tenant, but I can still see the ghost lettering of Hollywood Video on the storefront, brighter gray spaces against the gray stucco exterior.

I can see Calvin too, dimly, through the window. I park my Corolla and take a deep breath. I don't know how jazzed Dad would be about me meeting a guy at the Game Shack after closing hours. This is why I told him and Mom that I was going to a movie with my coworker Michelle instead. It's an improbable story—Michelle is thirty-something and the mother of three young kids—but they appeared to believe me. As well they should have. As far as they know, I have never lied to them.

A bell rings when I enter the store. The aisles of DVDs and VHS tapes have been replaced with shelves of board games and playing cards. A series of circular tables runs down the center of the store. Calvin is seated at one of the tables, idly moving around the pieces to a board game. Call me sentimental, but I half expected to see Calvin dressed in a cummerbund, vest, and bow tie. Instead, he is dressed in jeans and a plain white T-shirt, and is wearing a name tag that says "Brad."

"What happened to Calvin?" I say, sitting across from him and flicking the name tag lightly with my finger.

"That was kind of a high school thing."

I suddenly feel irrelevant. After all, I am kind of a high school thing too.

"You go by Calvin on Facebook."

Calvin shrugs. "Old habits die hard."

"Well, Bradley," I say, trying for a flirtatious tone, "what did you ask me here for? Do you need help closing out the register?"

Calvin looks across the table at me in *that way*, and my stomach tightens like a fist. I know exactly why he's asked me here. We have some unfinished business from last night.

"I think I can handle it," Calvin says. "Although, if I did need help, you'd be the first person I'd ask."

"I did ace precalc," I say, referring to the class we shared in high school.

"I remember. You were the smartest girl in that class."

"Try student."

He doesn't bother to correct himself. Instead, he reaches for the stack of playing cards on the table and gives them an impressive shuffle.

"Do you like playing games, Sabrina?" The cards in Calvin's hands collapse from an arched bridge into a neat, tidy pile.

"Depends on the game." I study the rather elaborate game board in front of me and then meet his gaze. "Do you?"

"When I win." He flashes me a smile worthy of the

Cheshire Cat. Then his cell phone beeps, stealing his attention away from me. He grins as he reads a text message, and I am unaccountably envious of the sender.

"It's Alex," he says, his thumbs flying as he types back a response, "checking up on me."

"Alex?"

"My friend from Game Club," he says, clueing me in. It's silly, but I'm relieved. In my mind, I picture Alex as one of those walking stereotypes with greasy hair and a black trench coat. Alex is probably the kind of guy who grew up playing Dungeons and Dragons in a stale, windowless basement. I can compete with Alex.

"Why couldn't he close the store tonight?" I ask. "Comic book convention?"

Calvin gives me an odd little smile, as if I've said something wrong.

"Something like that." His cell phone beeps again, and he forgets me entirely as he thumbs out another text. I pretend to be enthralled by the board game on the table, although I can't make any sense of it.

"So," I say, the moment Calvin places his phone down, "presiding over Game Club must keep you pretty busy."

"Not really. Alex does most of the work. That's one of the reasons I don't mind filling in for her at the store once in a while."

He doesn't mind filling in for *her*? My mind buzzes as I swap my mental picture of Alex from a Dungeons and Dragons grease ball to a Kim Kardashian type with the brain of Marie Curie. I can't compete with Alex. This is obvious. Even though I am here in the flesh, Calvin can't keep his eyes off his phone.

I wasn't exactly sure what I expected tonight, but I certainly hadn't planned on being ignored. I have the sudden impulse to bolt for the door. My body language must alert Calvin of my imminent departure, because he suddenly looks away from his phone and turns his attention back to me.

"Alex is just whining about her psych paper," Calvin says. "That's why she pawned her shift off on me tonight. The thing's due Monday, and she's just now getting started on it."

"Oh," I say, with a good deal of effort. My mouth is so dry that, at the moment, I'm lucky to manage saying even this.

"I took the class last semester," Calvin continues, "so she thinks I have all the answers or something."

"Are you majoring in psychology?" I say after I manage to dislodge my tongue from the roof of my mouth.

"I haven't declared yet. I've petitioned Boise State to pursue an interdisciplinary degree, but I'm still waiting for approval."

"An interdisciplinary degree?"

"It's like a customized degree. The school allows it if you can demonstrate that one course of study doesn't meet your particular educational needs. My degree, hopefully, will be comprised of coursework in anthropology, psychology, and philosophy."

"Geez, Calvin, you really don't like limits, do you?"

"I just want what I want." He zones in on me with his eyes and my stomach tightens into a fist again, only this time, it starts pummeling my lungs too. "What about you? Why biology?"

I'm not sure I can even breathe, let alone talk, but somehow I force myself to answer his question.

"Because biology has solutions."

"What kind of solutions?"

"Solutions to nature's accidents. Like malaria. Or cancer."

Calvin raises an eyebrow. "Or unwanted pregnancies?"

I shift in my seat. "Look, the way I see it, people are a lot happier when things go according to plan. When mistakes are minimized. The world is disordered, but it doesn't necessarily have to be. If you can understand life, you can understand how to perfect it."

"So that's it, Sabrina? You're going to get a degree in biology, and then what? Rid the world of imperfection?"

"I'm not that idealistic. But I'm also not fond of the way nature's little accidents wreak havoc on people's lives."

"Wreak havoc. That's such a weird expression. I mean, is anything other than havoc wrought?"

"Iron." It thrills me to no end that this response makes Calvin laugh. He laughs, and then he sighs, and then things get pretty quiet. I struggle to breathe under the blanket of Calvin's gaze. It is not lost on me that, unlike last night, tonight we are technically alone. The doors are locked; the store is empty. It's just Calvin and me, hidden among the towering shelves of board games.

I lean forward in my chair, my whole body tingling with the pleasure of anticipation. This is the point where he's supposed to, you know, make a move. I imagine how the press of Calvin's lips against mine will feel like a tender stamp of approval.

I stare at Calvin, positively aching for him, admiring the contrast of his dark hair and his bright, blue eyes, and I can almost feel what it's like to be intentionally wanted. And I realize that I didn't only lie to my parents tonight—I lied to myself. I didn't just come here for a kiss. I came for validation.

Except, the only move Calvin makes is to reach for his phone again. He does this in an off-handed kind of way, like I'm not sitting expectantly across from him, struggling to breathe.

"It's Alex again," he says. "Can you give me a minute?"

I shrug acquiescence and wait as Calvin participates in a texting mini-marathon. To pass the time, I arrange the plastic pawns in front of me in a neat line and then knock them down, one at a time. Calvin is not distracted by this mildly aggressive behavior. He focuses on what appears to be a rather intense exchange with Alex until, finally, he slips his phone into his pocket.

"Sorry," Calvin says. "Alex has absolutely no idea what she's doing."

That makes two of us.

"I might have to cut out early tonight. Alex needs some serious help with that paper."

Instantly I stand and, on wobbly legs, head for the doors, which, of course, are locked.

"I don't have to leave right now," Calvin says, cocking his head toward me as I fumble with an impossible lock.

"Well I do." I fold my arms and wait for Calvin to help me open the door. He shakes his head and then easily flips the lock and swings the door open. Calvin at least has the courtesy to walk me to my car. The lights in the parking lot are bright and theatrical, and I feel exposed and vulnerable, like an actor under a spotlight. When we reach my Corolla, Calvin takes a look at my bumper sticker, the one that says "Drive Carefully—90% of People Are Caused by Accidents," and lets out a low whistle.

"You've really labeled yourself, haven't you, Sabrina?"

When I don't respond, he gently puts his hand on my shoulder.

"Alex is just a friend."

"Whatever." Frankly, Alex is the last person I want to talk about right now. "I think my dad saw you last night," I say, changing the subject. "He asked me about my 'stalker' the minute he got home."

"That's good," Calvin says, smiling.

"Well, yeah. Only . . ."

"What?"

"Well, what if I don't end up going to Caltech? What if I stay here?"

I'm being intentionally vague, but Calvin's a smart guy. He knows what I'm talking about. How are things going to, you know, *work* if my dad thinks he's some skeezy stalker? But if Calvin's concerned that posing as my stalker may jeopardize our future, he doesn't let it show.

"Sabrina." He reaches for me and gives my hand a sympathetic squeeze. I wait for him to say more, to smother me with his gaze, to take me into his arms and kiss me. But he doesn't do any of these things. "I've got to wrap some things up," he says, letting go of my hand. Then he turns from me and starts walking back to the store.

I wait until I'm in my car to start crying. Like he said, Calvin wants what he wants. And he doesn't want me.

Chapter 8

During dinner on Monday, Heather makes an announcement.

"Sabrina," she says, glancing at me over a rather elaborate bowl of fruit, "I've scheduled you an appointment with Paul tomorrow."

"What?"

"Paul noticed you missed your last checkup." She pauses to take a bite of Mom's chicken and broccoli casserole. "I mentioned you had tomorrow off, and he said he could fit you into the schedule." She sees the sour expression on my face and tries to sweeten the deal by adding, "He even said he'll waive your co-pay."

I pretend not to notice that Dad's eyes light up when she says this.

"Geez, Heathcliff, don't you and Paul have anything better to talk about than my dental care?"

Heather, as usual, ignores me. But it's obvious she's not done with the announcements, because she puts her fork down and kind of straightens herself up on her chair. "More important," she says, "Paul has invited all of us over for dinner tomorrow night."

"Heather!" Mom exclaims. She looks like she's about to pass out from the sheer giddiness of the news.

"It's not that exciting, Mom," Heather says, but her radiant smile betrays her.

"Will you be seeing Paul tonight?" Dad asks.

"No. Paul volunteers at the dental clinic downtown on Mondays."

"Wow, Heather, I didn't know you were dating Mother Theresa," I say. Apparently, no one cares about what I have to say, because this comment does nothing to dampen the mood. Everyone, even Mack and The Noise, continues to wear these huge, moronic smiles on their faces, no doubt thinking about how wonderful life is now that Paul's shown up, wielding a braided leather belt and waiving co-pays left and right.

In fairness, I cannot blame my bad mood entirely on Paul the Great. Ever since Calvin basically rejected me, I have been kind of a basket case. I push a cube of cantaloupe around on my plate, waiting for my family to ride out the wave of excitement that Heather's announcement has unfurled, and try not to think about how bleak my future is now that both Calvin and Caltech are pretty much out of the picture.

"Sabrina," Mom says suddenly, noticing me for what must be the first time tonight, "is it necessary for you to wear that hat at the dinner table?"

"Yes." I emphatically adjust the brim of my safari hat. Of course, it is not necessary that I wear my hat at the dinner table. It is also not necessary for me to go to the dentist tomorrow, because I have impeccable brushing habits and have never once had a cavity. Most of the things I do are not, in fact, necessary, but I do them anyway.

Dinner winds down and we settle into our Monday night routine. Dad takes the kids out front to kick a soccer ball around in the yard, and Mom and Heather sink into the couch to watch another round of survival of the dimmest. I check Facebook. Of course, Calvin has still not responded to the message I sent him Saturday night, the one where I requested never to be seen by him again. Of course, his lack of a response devastates me. I try to distract myself by chatting with Cleverbot, but my heart's not in it. I type *Is it ever necessary to wear a safari hat to the dinner table?*, but close the app before Cleverbot responds.

The theme song for *The Bachelorette* summons my attention. A montage of photographs of Jordan Greene flashes across the screen as I enter the family room. I join Mom and Heather on the couch and succumb to the mind-numbing agent that is reality TV.

And then two unrelated but equally unexpected things happen.

The first shouldn't come as such a surprise. I mean, the network has been hyping tonight's episode of *The Bachelorette* as "shocking." Commercials have aired all week luring viewers with clips of Jordan Greene looking, well, shocked, as she receives a visit from, ahem, "a mystery man." The mystery man's face is, of course, scrambled, but still, you can see his body. So tonight, as we watch Jordan open the door of some swanky hotel room to reveal Thayne Stockett on the other side, we shouldn't gasp in, well, shock. Because really, we all should have seen this coming. Even with his face obscured, Thayne's body kind of gives his identity away.

The show's host, Chris Harrison, introduces Thayne and announces that, for the first time ever, a new contestant will be added to the show mid-season. Mr. Harrison describes this decision as "groundbreaking," which is just a nice way of saying that the remaining four contestants are anything but interesting. Then he recedes into the space outside of the camera's eye, leaving Thayne's imposing figure in the open doorway.

We watch in disbelief as Thayne waltzes into the room and basically confesses his undying love for Jordan. He can't let her continue doing the show, he says, without letting her know his "true feelings." At one point, Jordan starts crying. The whole thing feels forced and scripted. Thayne whisks Jordan into his arms and the scene devolves into a full-on make-out session. Somehow, I manage to tear my eyes from the screen and peek over at Heather. She doesn't look so good. This may be the first time in my life I've seen someone literally turn green with envy.

As soon as the show cuts to commercial, we all start talking at once.

Heather says, "I have to throw up."

Mom says, "Thank goodness Mack didn't see that."

I say, "They actually look kind of good together." And they do. Thayne's bulging biceps complement Jordan's sculpted abs. They are tan, blonde, and completely superficial—like life-sized Barbie and Ken dolls.

But Heather doesn't want to hear this. The truth, as everyone knows, hurts.

"They do not," Heather says, "look good together." She rests her head in her hands. I inch away from her, afraid that she is literally going to vomit on my shoes.

"It was probably all staged, anyway," I say, trying to soften the effect of my previous comment.

"That," Heather says, sitting up and pointing violently at the TV, "was as real as Jordan's tan. It's got to be a publicity stunt," she continues, "a way to hike up ratings. Doesn't it?"

She turns to me and Mom in desperation, but before either of us can reassure her, the front door slams. Dad races into the living room, harried and wild-eyed, Brodie in his arms and Mack at his side. His hands are trembling and his forehead is beaded with sweat. He looks literally sick with worry.

Dad focuses his wild eyes directly on me. And then the second unexpected event of the night happens.

"Sabrina," he says in a shaky voice, "we need to call the police."

Chapter 9

A prescient thought flashes through my mind, and I'd be willing to bet that Dad's meltdown has something to do with Calvin. I pull my safari hat down to cover my face, which I'm certain has literally gone white with dread, and silently will the couch cushions to engulf me.

"What is it, Don?" Mom says, her voice sharp with concern.

"It's that man. The one in the Escort. He just drove past the house again."

"What man?" Heather says. I suppose that, really, I should be the one asking this question. After all, Dad's statement was directed at me. But I don't need to ask this question. I know exactly who the guy in the Escort is. It's absurd, but a flicker of hope rises within me, and I wonder if, miracle of miracles, it is possible that Calvin still wants me.

This slight hope quickly flames out and gives way to nausea. Dad is going to call the cops on Calvin. My impulse to vomit is followed by an even stronger impulse to stop Dad from making the call. Or, more accurately, to stop Dad from making the call without exposing myself as a liar.

"Some lanky guy with a beard," Dad says. "Your mom

and I saw him Friday night too. We think it might be the same person who's been watching Sabrina at work. What do you think, Sabrina," Dad says, turning to me. "Does that sound like the same person to you?"

All eyes are on me, waiting for my answer. For once, being the center of attention does not thrill me. I dumbly stare back at my family, silently running through my options. If I say yes, I will not only put Calvin at risk, I'll threaten our chance at a relationship. If I say no, I will destroy perhaps the only shot I have at getting to Caltech.

Of course, there is a third option. I could confess the whole thing right now. If I had more time to think things through, I'd like to think that this is the choice I would make. I'd like to think that I'm still capable of doing the right thing.

But I don't have time to think things through. Under the pressure of my family's collective stare, I nod, because it is the head motion that requires the least amount of energy. Dad collapses onto the love seat, upsetting Brodie in the process. Brodie starts wailing, but instead of comforting him, Dad just vacantly sets him down on the floor.

"For heaven's sake, Don, don't be so dramatic," Mom says.

Apparently, Dad's not the only one prone to theatrics. Because just then *The Bachelorette* comes back from commercial break, and as the lust-fest between Thayne and Jordan resumes, Heather kind of yelps in pain and hides her head in her hands.

"It's Daddy!" Mack says, pointing at the screen.

It is obvious that someone needs to turn off the TV. It is obvious that someone needs to pick up The Noise, who is screaming at full capacity. It is also obvious that neither

Dad, Heather, nor I am capable of doing anything at the moment.

Mom, as the only functioning member of the family, stands up, picks up the baby, and resolutely turns off the TV. Then she purses her lips together and narrows her eyes at me. Things have just gone from bad to worse. Mom is taking charge.

"Sabrina," Mom says, "get me the nonemergency number for the police department."

This seems a little unnecessary. She does, after all, have her smart phone in hand and is perfectly capable of obtaining the number herself. It occurs to me that she may be challenging me, that she has seen through my stalker story this whole time.

I pull my phone from my pocket and google the Boise Police Department.

"Read me the number," Mom says.

I take a deep breath. This is the point of no return.

"The number, Sabrina."

I exhale and then read off the number. Mom punches the number into her phone, the sharp tips of her manicured nails clicking against the screen.

"I'd like to report an incident," Mom says into the phone. We all listen as she provides a brief description of Calvin and his car. She is silent for a moment, listening to the dispatcher, and then she cocks her head toward Dad.

"Don," she says, "did you get the plate number?"

Dad looks at her blankly, and Mom just shrugs, as if she's disappointed, but not surprised.

"No, we don't have the plate number," Mom says. I silently praise Dad's blessed oversight. Without a license plate number, what can the police really do?

I glance at Dad and give him a half-hearted smile. Poor Dad. He still looks pretty shaken up. It's terrible, but I can't help thinking that maybe this night hasn't been such a disaster after all. Maybe now Dad really is worried enough about me to send me to Caltech.

Dad catches my eye, but he doesn't return my smile. And when he speaks, it is as if he has read my mind.

"This is why we can't have you running off to some school hundreds of miles away. What if something like this happened there? Who would look out for you then?"

You would think that this is the worst thing I could hear right now. You would think this, but you would be wrong. Because when Mom finishes the call, she manages to hit me with something much, much worse.

"Well," Mom says, folding her arms across her chest, "the dispatcher suggested that, given the circumstances, you file a restraining order."

"But we don't have a plate number," I say.

"The zoo has that man's membership information." Mom preempts any argument I might make by narrowing her eyes at me. "You said so yourself, Sabrina. The dispatcher said once we have his name and address, all we have to do is go to the courthouse and fill out some paperwork."

She says this like filing a restraining order is some terribly mundane task, like setting the table or taking out the garbage. I stare helplessly at Mom, wondering how on earth I am going to get out of this mess.

"Sabrina," Mom says, "the next time you're at work, I want you to get this man's information. Then we'll go file the restraining order together."

Before I can respond to this impossible demand, my cell phone beeps. I furtively read a text message from Calvin that says: *Bet Daddy's scared now.*

My poor, sweet Calvin. You have no idea.

Chapter 10

A waiting room is the perfect place to be assaulted by your guilt.

I find this out Tuesday morning as I wait to be seen by Dr. Paul Nelson for an unsolicited and completely unnecessary dental exam. I reach for one of the dog-eared magazines splayed across the coffee table and idly flip to an article titled "Cemetery Caters to Golfers." My eyes scan the page, but even a story as bizarre as this cannot distract me from the persistent and plaguing thought that I am, quite simply, a terrible person.

I lied about Caltech, then I lied about being stalked, and now I have committed to give Mom Calvin's name and address. I am miserably caught in that proverbial tangled web of lies. Like a fly. The Fly. Somehow, I have transformed into something pretty hideous, despite my best-laid plans.

I have not heard from Calvin since he texted me last night. Of course, I haven't tried contacting him again, either. I thought I had made it pretty clear that I didn't want to see him anymore, so why did he drive past my house? Did he want to see me? Or was he hoping to ensure that I really do go to Caltech so he won't have to deal with me anymore?

I shouldn't be thinking about Calvin anyway. At the

moment, I have bigger fish to fry. I have to think of a way to avoid filing a restraining order. I also have to devise a new plan to get to Caltech. Unfortunately, the only solutions I can think of all involve the telling of more lies. I can already feel the sticky strands of deceit tightening around me, pinning me down.

I stand, ostensibly to stretch my legs, but really to convince myself that the lies I've told haven't completely immobilized me. I wander over to the Wall of Fame and easily spot my photo among the dozens of other children flashing cavity-free smiles. The picture was taken back when I was eight, back when I hadn't done anything wrong. Back when all I had to do to prove myself was ace a spelling test or brush my teeth.

I can't help but feel a little envious of my former self. It's silly, but part of me wishes I were her again. The girl in the photo practically radiates innocence, and as I study her guiltless face, I realize that there's something I want more than going to Caltech or dating Calvin. More than anything, I don't want my parents to know I've lied to them. They can't know I'm a terrible person. I resolve to do anything to keep them from finding me out—even if it means telling more lies. Their approval is worth lying for.

A hygienist peers into the waiting room and calls my name. I follow her into an examination room and confidently sit in the dental chair. I may be a terrible person, but I still have faultless teeth. That has to count for something.

I drum my fingers on the armrest as the hygienist cleans my teeth. I rinse and spit like a pro. I don't flinch when the hygienist armors me with a lead apron before taking an X-ray of my teeth. This checkup may be entirely unnecessary, but I find myself enjoying the process. There's something reassuring in taking a test I know I'll pass.

The hygienist ushers me back into the exam room while the film develops. A few minutes later Paul appears in the doorway, clipboard in hand, wearing navy Crocs and a white lab coat with his name embroidered above the pocket. I resist telling him that 2005 called and wants its Crocs back. I resist asking him if he needs to refill his prescription for Rogaine. I just sit in the chair and beam at him, the ideal patient that I am, and wait to be pronounced perfect.

"Sabrina." Paul's voice exudes warmth. He sits down on the rolling stool beside me and takes a cursory glance at my chart. "Glad we were able to get you in today. Now tell me, did Barb waive your co-pay?"

I nod and Paul gives me a million-dollar smile.

"Good. I want to make sure you're getting the family discount."

Gag me.

"I'm looking forward to tonight," Paul says.

"Me too." I try not to squirm in my chair. In the midst of all the chaos that occurred last night, I'd nearly forgotten Paul's dinner invitation.

"So, Heather says you're planning on attending Boise State in the fall. You looking forward to that?"

"I guess."

"Heather also told me you'll be on scholarship."

"Yeah." I should probably leave my answer at this, but I can't help myself. "I have a scholarship to Caltech too."

"Pretty and smart," Paul says. "Just like your sister."

This is too much. I forget that I'm playing the role of ideal patient and pull a face.

"I'm not like Heather."

"Of course you are," Paul says, placing the clipboard in his lap and giving me a good once-over. "Beauty takes many forms."

Nice try, Croc man.

Emboldened by my indignation, I decide to turn the tables on Paul and start questioning him.

"What's the deal with you and Heather anyway? I mean, you've dated for, like, a whole week . . ."

"And?"

"And suddenly I'm getting the family discount?"

Paul shrugs and gets this goofy look on his face.

"When it's right, it's right." Thankfully, he declines to elaborate on this platitude. Instead, he snaps on a pair of plastic gloves, selects a mouth mirror and probe from a tray of shiny instruments, and scoots toward me.

"Open for me." I, of course, oblige. He looms over me, poking and prodding along my gum line, waxing poetic about Heather and all she's gone through. I swear, from the way he's talking, I'm surprised Lifetime hasn't offered to make a biopic movie of Heather's life. But unless stupidity qualifies as a hardship, I have no idea what Paul's talking about. Fortunately, my present condition spares me from having to respond.

Finally, Paul finishes his monologue. "Everything looks good." He peels off the plastic gloves and tosses them in the trash. "Except for a small cavity on one of your back molars, you're nearly perfect."

"Except for what?" I say, sitting straight up.

"You have a cavity," Paul says, his voice slow and deliberate. "On your lower left molar."

"But I've never had a cavity."

"It's nothing to worry about. We'll have you back in a few weeks to get it filled, and then you'll be good as new."

"I want to see the film."

"What?"

"I want to see the film," I say, louder this time.

As if humoring a child, Paul unclips the film from the board and hands it to me. I scan the ghostly white picture of my teeth, trying to make sense of the image. Once it's clear that I'm not going to locate the cavity on my own, Paul leans over and deftly points to the molar in question. My eyes follow the arrow of his finger to an inky black mark on the film.

For the rest of the day I am haunted by the vision of that small, but certain, sign of decay.

Chapter 11

We are huddled together on Paul's front porch like would-be trick-or-treaters, costumed as the perfect family. The word "coif" comes to mind—and I'm not just talking about us women. Heather has teased so much gel into Mack's fine blonde hair it's as if he's wearing a hair helmet. Or a mace. I inch away from Mack so as not to puncture myself on one of his sharp, stiff spikes of hair, wondering if there isn't something willfully aggressive about the way Heather's transformed him into a weapon. Love is a battlefield, indeed.

Heather reaches for the doorbell with her manicured hand, but just before she pushes the bell, she stalls.

"Don't," Heather says, glancing at us over her shoulder, "talk about my past."

This is, like, the ninetieth time she's said this tonight. But now there's a hint of desperation in her voice that makes it sound more like a plea than a warning. Obviously, her nerves are still raw from witnessing Thayne's surprise appearance on *The Bachelorette*. We nod reassurance, and Heather takes a deep breath and rings the bell.

Paul promptly answers the door and herds us inside. He rattles off our names like he's calling roll: Heather, Don,

Cindy, Sabrina, Mack, Brodie. We remain in a tight cluster in the entryway, scoping out Paul's pad while exchanging polite greetings. This place makes our 1970s Cape Cod seem cramped and drab in comparison. It is an obscenely large house for one single man, a fact that Mom is only too eager to point out.

"The only thing this home doesn't have," Mom says, "is a family." The line sounds terribly rehearsed—even for Mom, who, as a realtor, is well-versed in rehearsed. But Paul isn't put off by the comment. Instead, as if reading from the same script, he puts his arm around Heather and looks directly into her eyes.

"I think I know how to fix that," he says, pulling Heather into him. The blush this comment brings to Heather's face only makes her look lovelier. Ugh. This level of gooeyness cannot continue. I rack my mind for something to say that will return this scene to something that resembles normal. And then, I notice Paul's shirt.

"Nice shirt," I say. The shirt in question is a white cotton polo with black horizontal stripes. There is nothing particularly noteworthy about this shirt. Only tonight, wonder of wonders, Dad is wearing the exact same one.

"Hey," Dad says, smiling at the similarity. "Costco?"

Paul gives Dad a double thumbs-up. "You're looking at a card-carrying member."

"I knew there was something I liked about you."

To my complete amazement, Heather does not drop dead from embarrassment. In fact, the wardrobe coincidence seems to merely amuse her. I try to imagine how this scenario would play out if Paul were any of Heather's former boyfriends, but then I stop myself. It is simply not possible that any of Heather's former boyfriends would ever show up anywhere dressed as Dad's identical twin.

Paul directs us into the living room, an airy, open space with vaulted ceilings and thick, spotless carpet. The only significant furniture in the room, other than a pair of leather couches, is a gigantic plasma TV. The TV is switched on to CNN, and as I admire Anderson Cooper's perfect hair, I wonder again what Heather is doing with Paul. I mean, the guy watches CNN. To my knowledge, the closest thing Heather's ever watched that resembles news is *Entertainment Tonight*.

The news crawl on the bottom of the screen reads "School-bus sized debris from defunct satellite may hit Earth." No one but me notices this rather ominous report. I wander through the pair of open French doors that lead to the deck and gaze up at the clear summer sky. At any moment, a broken satellite may hurtle down from space and strike me dead. I guess I shouldn't be surprised. Disasters have a tendency of striking from out of the blue.

The probability of that satellite hitting anyone, let alone me, has got to be ridiculously small. But I go back inside anyway, just in case. Paul is setting up the Wii for Mack. Mack holds the controller in his hands with something like reverence, listening intently to Paul's instructions. Despite the tutorial, Mack's skills prove to be considerably poor. Paul scoops Mack up in his lap, obviously unfazed by his aggressive hairstyle, and takes over for him. Mack gazes up at Paul, regarding him as some kind of god, and then settles into his lap with an ease that makes even me want to sigh with contentment.

"Need any help with dinner?" Mom asks.

"No, thank you," Paul says, shifting Mack off his lap. "It's about that time, though, isn't it? I bet the boys are getting hungry."

Mack doesn't look hungry, just disappointed that he is losing his gaming partner.

"Soup's on," Dad says, and we all shuffle after Paul into the kitchen, where we are greeted by an enormous paper bag from Cantonese Kitchen. Paul reaches into the bag and starts to scatter an assortment of Styrofoam food containers across the granite countertop.

"Take-out," he says by way of apology. "I don't cook."

"Just another reason you need a woman around here," Mom says. I think I can actually hear subtlety slam the door as it flees the premises. Heather doesn't cook either, but I refrain from volunteering this information. Mom isn't trying to tell the truth; she's trying to make a sale.

Without asking for Paul's permission, Mom opens a glass-paned cupboard and takes out several pretty ceramic bowls.

"If I've learned anything as a realtor, it's this," Mom says, deftly dumping the contents of the Styrofoam containers into the bowls. "Presentation matters." She sweeps the emptied containers off the counter and into the trash, fusses the bowls into an arrangement, and deals a serving spoon into each. To her credit, this transformation really does make the food look more appetizing.

"Wow, Cindy," Paul says, "that's magic."

We each take a turn dishing up and then find a seat at the table. Somehow, I have the unfortunate luck of sitting across from Heather and Paul. They angle their chairs together so they can look at each other, even though they're sitting side by side. Heather plants a hand on Paul's thigh, like she's trying to hold him in place. To me, this gesture is nothing but a waste of energy. I mean, I can see the guy's face. He's not going anywhere.

"You've got a great view of the valley here," Dad says.

"Isn't it fantastic?" Heather says.

"You can see the city's fireworks from the deck," Paul says. "If you guys don't have plans, you should come over this weekend for the Fourth."

"Sounds lovely," Mom says. Sounds lovely? What on earth has happened to my family? My parents and Paul make tentative plans for Friday night, roping me into yet another unsolicited meeting with my dentist. Paul notices the pained look on my face and offers me a sympathetic smile.

"Looks like you're still recovering from your bad news," he says.

"What bad news?" Dad says. Cue the hand wringing and heart palpitations.

"I have a cavity, Dad," I say, hoping no one notices the way my voice breaks when I say this.

"You have a cavity, Sabby-apple?" Now I'm certain I can never let Dad know I've lied to him. He is the very picture of astonished, and I've only confessed to dental decay.

"It's very minor," Paul says, clearly bewildered by the sudden tension in the room. In an attempt to negotiate his way around this baffling family dynamic, Paul shifts gears. "One of my patients told me a joke today."

I brace myself for the comedic antics of Dr. Paul Nelson.

"What does the dentist of the year get?" He waits a second and then, when no one attempts to answer, he delivers the punch line. "A little plaque."

"Oh, Paul," Heather says. "That's almost as bad as one of Dad's jokes." Then she does something that surprises us all. She starts to laugh. Not the kind of polite, forced laughter that usually follows the punch line of some dumb joke, but the kind of unrestrained, flowing laughter that accompanies delirious happiness. I can't remember if I've ever heard Heather laugh this way before. When she finally stops laughing, she turns to Paul and gives him the most radiant smile, and in return he tenderly brushes a strand of hair from her face and tucks it behind her ear.

Watching this exchange between Heather and Paul, I finally get it. This isn't about money for Heather. I'm not generous enough to say that Heather deserves Paul, but I'm smart enough to see that he would make her happy.

Brodie starts fussing, interrupting Heather and Paul's moment. Heather makes a show of standing, even though we all know Dad's the one who walks the baby during meals. But Paul beats him to the punch, leaping from his chair and scooping Brodie up in his arms with alarming speed. To our collective amazement, Brodie stops crying—although Paul's jarring bouncing probably has him more startled than soothed.

"Aren't genetics wild?" Paul says, tussling Brodie's dark brown hair. "I can't get over the differences between these two boys."

Mack is blonde and fair; Brodie is dark and olive-skinned. But there is nothing remarkable about this. Not if you've seen the baby daddies.

"Well, having different fathers has something to do with it," Mom says.

Paul stops bouncing the baby. Heather hangs her head. It is obvious Mom has said something wrong.

"Different fathers?" Paul says.

"He doesn't know?" Mom says to Heather.

"I was going to tell him, Mom," Heather says. Everyone notices the way her voice breaks when she says this.

"You were going to tell me what, Heather?"

"Paul, I . . ." Heather bites her lower lip to stop from crying. Brodie, however, knows no such trick and starts bawling at full capacity. Rather than resuming his jarring bouncing to soothe him again, Paul grimaces and, as if he's ridding himself of something distasteful, sets Brodie on the ground.

"Whose father were you married to?" Paul says, trying to puzzle the whole thing together.

"Married?" Mom says before Heather even has a chance to reply. "Heather's never been married."

Heather shoots Mom a searing look, which, despite everything, seems justified. She did, after all, repeatedly instruct us not to talk about her past. Then she pushes her chair back from the table and, rivaling Paul's own display of speed just moments earlier, rushes out of the kitchen and down the hall.

We are all astonished, but poor Paul actually looks like he's just been hit by a school bus–sized piece of debris.

Disaster usually comes from out of the blue, but sometimes you at least have the benefit of a news crawl to give you a heads up. It's clear that Paul was utterly unprepared for this blow. I wonder for a moment if he is going to keel over and collapse to the floor and start sobbing along with Brodie. We wait as Paul suffers through an agonizing moment of helplessness, and then, incredulously, watch as he staggers out of the kitchen and follows Heather down the hall.

Chapter 12

Needless to say, the drive home from Paul's is a bit strained.

Before we pile into Dad's Tahoe, I make a point of taking a good look at the impressive view of the valley from Paul's driveway, certain it will be my last. I climb into the car and head for the back seat, not wanting to be caught in the crossfire of the inevitable showdown that is about to occur between Heather and Mom. Mack joins me in the back and I help buckle him into his booster seat. The sharp spikes of his hair have wilted into limp curls, as if in admission of defeat. After what just occurred, Heather's defense seems glaringly weak. A mixture of hair gel and vague warnings was never going to be enough of a shield to stave off the truth.

Dad pulls out of the driveway and heads home. The AC is blasting and I adjust the vents so that the air hits me directly, although I can't tell if it's the heat or the silence that's making me uncomfortable. We are all engaged in a game of conversational chicken, wondering who has enough guts to step on the gas and speak first. Mom, of course, wins the game.

"Well, that didn't go as planned, did it Heather?"

"Cindy . . ." Mom bats Dad's protest away with a wave of her hand.

"What were you thinking?" Mom says, turning around in her seat to face Heather directly.

Clearly, Heather wasn't thinking. That's kind of the problem.

"What were you thinking, Heather?" Mom says again, louder this time. "I mean, did you really think Paul wasn't going to find out that you lied to him?"

I stare at the back of Heather's head, which is remarkably still given the fact that she is crying. I am surprised by the empathy I feel for her. She's not the only liar in the car. For perhaps the first time in my life, I can relate to Heather.

"He wouldn't have found out if you hadn't told him," Heather says.

"Don't blame what just happened on me!" Mom says.

"I told you not to talk about my past." Heather's voice is barely audible. Even she knows this is a weak argument. "And I didn't lie to Paul. He just assumed things."

"You let him believe those assumptions," Mom says.

"I had to. Paul would never have gone out with a girl like me."

"Now, Heather," Dad says.

"It's true." In light of the way we were just summarily dismissed from Paul's home, no one can really argue with this statement.

Thankfully, Mom stops reaming Heather and turns back around. She obviously has her own wounds to nurse— she was nearly as smitten with Paul as Heather was. As a realtor, she shouldn't have been taken in so easily. After all, isn't she the one who always says if a deal seems too good to be true, it probably is?

We continue to drive home in relative silence. That is, until my cell phone beeps.

"Who is it?" Heather asks, hope rising in her voice.

I fish my phone out of my purse and find that I have a text message from Calvin.

"It's not Paul," I say. I'd like to say the burst of empathy I've just felt for Heather precludes me from smiling as I read Calvin's message. But even though my sister is practically in mourning, my heart still flutters with joy as I read the words: *I need to see you again.*

—*That can be arranged.*

—*Locash?*

Location, location. Where do I dare to see Calvin again? Definitely not the house. Or the Game Shack. If I'm going to see Calvin again, I want it to be on my own turf.

—*Zoo. Tomorrow. Noon.*

"Who is it?" Heather says again.

"Michelle," I say, tucking my phone back in my purse. "From work."

For a moment, I'm worried about making a reference to work around Mom. I wait for her to turn around and remind me to get my stalker's info from admin tomorrow. But she doesn't say anything. And I know it's kind of ridiculous, but her lack of a response starts to make me mad. How is it that she has forgotten me completely? I understand that this whole business with Heather and Paul has her upset, but as far as she knows, my very life is in danger.

Then again, I'm not the one crying. The sound of

Heather's stifled sobs accompanies our entire drive home. When Dad finally pulls into the garage and we file inside, her face is so swollen she is almost unrecognizable. She slumps into a chair and hides her bloated face in her hands. We circle around her, not sure what to say. Finally, Heather raises her head and stares vacantly in front of her.

"I'm tired of living with my mistakes," Heather says.

"You're not the only one," Mom says. Oddly enough, she looks at me when she says this. Maybe I'm being sensitive, but I can't help feeling like she has just made a veiled reference to me.

Chapter 13

YこOu have a stalker," Michelle whispers in my ear. I have just concluded a presentation on owls and the small crowd gathered around me is in the process of disbanding. Snowy, the zoo's resident barn owl, is still perched on my arm, and as I crane my head in search of said stalker, I envy her extra vertebrae. You know, the whole 270-degree rotation thing.

"Where?" I say.

"Over there." Michelle points to the concrete terrace by the Oasis. "The guy in the blue shirt."

I look toward the terrace, fully expecting to see Calvin. But the guy she's pointing at is definitely not Calvin. Unlike Calvin, the guy in the blue shirt is conventionally handsome. He is blonde and athletic and, even from a distance, I can tell he has the kind of teeth that Dr. Paul Nelson couldn't find fault with. The guy looks like an Olympian. I fully expect the national anthem to start playing at any moment.

"He looks like one of the Winklevoss twins," I say. And then, I state the obvious. "Guys like that don't look at girls like me."

Michelle gives me a good once-over and then huffs out a laugh.

"You're right. Men never look at pretty young girls with great legs."

I reflexively look down at my completely unremarkable legs. Michelle's comment only confirms what I have long suspected: she is, indeed, delusional.

"I wouldn't mind if he were looking at me," Michelle says. "Heck, I wouldn't mind if anyone looked at me. Enjoy it while it lasts, Sabrina. I'm telling you, once you have that first baby, everything goes downhill." Michelle has a way of making married with children seem beyond pathetic.

"That guy's not looking at me." But if I'm being truthful, I have to admit, it kind of looks like he's looking at me.

"Unless that guy's really into birds, he's looking at you."

"Some people are really into birds, Michelle."

She, of all people, should know this. We do, in fact, work at the zoo, with people who are really into all kinds of animals. I mean, one of our coworkers just authored a full-length book on the coral king snake. For fun.

As if determined to prove me wrong, the guy in the blue shirt starts walking toward us. Michelle squeezes my arm and then ducks away. As my unremarkable legs turn to jelly, I silently curse her for abandoning me. I want to run away after her, but even if I could make my legs cooperate with me, it's too late. Captain America's already here, flashing his perfect teeth at me. I have the strangest impulse to salute him. That or place my hand on my heart and recite the pledge. Thankfully, I do neither and manage a weak smile.

Then it hits me. I've seen this guy before. He was around the day I had the star shell tortoise out. This is the cute guy who inspired my whole stalker story. I cannot for the life of me figure out what he could possibly want from me now. So I do the obvious thing and ask him.

"What do you want?" I say.

"I want to talk to you."

This is, frankly, unbelievable.

"You want to talk to me?"

"About the owl." He breaks eye contact with me and focuses on Snowy instead. Of course he is here to talk about the barn owl. My presence is merely incidental.

"These beautiful birds have a history of nesting in barn lofts and church steeples," I say, seeking cover in my talking points. "Although it wasn't until 1769 that an Italian naturalist coined the name barn owl. Other names for the barn owl are monkey-faced owl, church owl, hobgoblin owl . . ." I continue to rattle off a list of names, almost forgetting that the poster boy for capitalism and corn-fed beef is standing in front of me. Almost, but not completely. Good looks like his are hard to ignore.

"I prefer *Tyto alba*," he says, interrupting me.

I leave off my recitation in astonishment. Did this guy really just name Snowy's genus and species? Oh say can you see. Captain America is kind of a nerd.

"She's incredible," he says, keeping his gorgeous eyes locked on Snowy.

"Lucky guess."

"Well, it's an educated guess." And then, he turns his gorgeous eyes on me. "The dense spotting on her breast identifies her sex."

I don't know which word has me blushing more—breast or sex. Of course, there's no reason for me to be flustered. Clearly, this guy is into the bird and not me. As a realtor's daughter, I know as well as anyone that if a deal seems too good to be true, it probably is. And the deal that involves me and a Winklevoss twin doppelganger with a keen interest in ornithology isn't just too good to be true. It is pure fantasy.

"I should get going," I say, glancing at Snowy. "My arm is killing me."

"I bet." I wait for him to walk away, but the guy just stands there, like he's waiting for something. Finally he turns, but before he even takes a step he flips back around and faces me again.

"Hey, look, I'm sorry if I was kind of obnoxious just now. You know, with all the bird talk. Really, I'm just glad I finally got a chance to talk to you."

This is too much.

"You, sir, are a credit to Miss Manners." I know. It's kind of a snarky thing to say. But I can't help myself.

"I'm not being polite. It's hard to get you alone. You always have, like, a throng of people around you."

"It's not me who's drawing the crowd." I place my unoccupied hand on my safari hat in a vain attempt to stop my mind from wobbling.

"I wouldn't be so sure. In fact, it looks like some guy's stalking you right now."

"Who?"

"Over there." He points behind me toward the Primate House. "The guy with the beard."

I turn toward the Primate House and, sure enough, Calvin is parked on a bench, looking at me. This, of course, is completely expected, as I was the one who asked him to come here. I feel a pang of guilt as it dawns on me that I had forgotten to look for him. But even this pang of guilt isn't enough to override the sudden impulse I have to lie.

"That guy's not looking at me," I say, even though Calvin is most definitely looking at me. As if determined to prove me wrong, Calvin waves.

"I'm pretty sure that guy's looking at you," Captain America says.

"Fine. You're right. He's a . . ." I stall for a moment, searching for the right term. "Friend."

"Right." His eyes dart to the name tag pinned to my uniform. "I'll let you go now. Sabrina." He gives me one more dazzling smile before he walks away. I tell myself that I should be thankful he is gone. Now I can focus my energy where it belongs—on Calvin. I take a deep breath and walk across the lawn toward the Primate House. Calvin sees me coming but he doesn't bother to budge from the bench.

"Hey," I say when I finally reach him. I am a little breathless from my trek, and my right arm is burning from holding Snowy for so long.

"What do you know? It's the Lord of the Wings."

"That's me." I am startled that he has committed a line from my Facebook page to memory. Has he been studying my profile, pining for me? Or does he just have the freak ability to retain useless information?

"So who was that?"

"Who was who?" I say, although I know perfectly well who he's talking about.

"The guy with the hair."

"Just some guy." This, at least, is an honest answer. After all, I don't even know Captain America's name. "Do you want to help me put Snowy away?" I say, hoping to change the subject. "I know you're dying to see behind the 'Staff Only' doors."

"I'm good."

This is not the reception I was expecting. After all, Calvin's the one who sent me a text last night that said he *needed* to see me. Only now that he's seeing me, his body language isn't saying "need." It's saying something more like "mild annoyance."

"How was your date with Alex the other night?"

"It wasn't a date."

"Then what was it?"

"Sabrina, I'm not here to talk about Alex. I'm just here to settle up."

"Settle up?"

"Yeah. I finished the job and I'm here to collect my fifty bucks."

He may as well have just punched me in the gut. I place my free hand on the bench to steady myself. And then, because I can't think of anything else to say, I drop a line I used just moments earlier. Only, this time, it's completely insincere.

"You, sir, are a credit to Miss Manners."

"I'm not trying to be a tool, Sabrina. It's just, something's come up, and I need the cash."

"I don't have the money." I kind of figured our little business deal was null and void when I explicitly asked Calvin to stop driving past my house. But then Calvin stands up and narrows his big blue eyes into impossibly small slits.

"I mean, I have the money. It's just not on me." I back step away from Calvin. The guy's unpredictable. I'm not sure I want to get acquainted with his particular brand of anger. Calvin moves toward me and I flinch.

"I'm not going to hurt you, Sabrina," he says, playfully punching my arm. "You can get me the money later."

"Okay." I wistfully glance back toward the concrete terrace by the Oasis, wondering why I terminated my previous conversation in exchange for this one. I would go back if I could, but Captain America has long since morphed into the crowd. He is gone, and as much I would like to inhabit fantasyland, I have to deal with the reality in front of me.

"Can you meet me tomorrow at Starbucks?" I say. "Around five, after my shift? I'll have the money then."

"Sure." This assurance of payment seems to improve Calvin's mood. He relaxes his shoulders and lets his long, skinny arms dangle at his side. I remind myself that I find these gangly limbs irresistible. Calvin is still looming over me, zoning in on me with his eyes, and I can't help thinking that something about his story doesn't add up.

"Calvin, why didn't you save yourself the twelve dollar admission fee and just ask me for the money on the phone?"

"Because I didn't pay the twelve dollar admission fee."

"Then how did you get in here?"

"This place is surprisingly easy to sneak into." He cracks

a wicked smile and then playfully punches my arm. "Do you still want my help locking this bird up?"

"I'm good." I am suddenly too exhausted to spend any more time with Calvin. Still, before I head for the Small Animal House, I somehow find the energy to take the long way and walk past the Oasis. I try to convince myself that I'm not looking for anyone in particular, but my eyes are as startlingly wide and alert as the owl's on my arm.

Chapter 14

Before I leave for work Thursday morning, Mom finally decides to remember me.

"Sabrina," she says as I rifle through the cupboard for a box of cereal, "my three o'clock cancelled on me today, so I'm free to go with you this afternoon."

"You're free to go where?" I seize a box of Cocoa Pebbles and turn to Mom with glazed eyes.

"To the courthouse."

Ah, yes. The courthouse. Where I will file a restraining order on my nonexistent stalker. It is definitely too early in the morning for me to deal with this. Mom, however, looks ready to deal with anything. It is hardly a quarter past eight, yet Mom is already dressed (in a sundress and heels, no less), aproned, and in the process of decorating a cake. I focus my bleary eyes on a colander of berries, rinsed and draining on a paper towel on the counter, and then on Mom, who is meticulously stabbing one berry after another into the white frosted cake to form the first stripe of the American Flag.

"What's the cake for?"

"I thought we'd barbeque tomorrow." I spy a pot of potatoes boiling on the stove and a pound of ground beef thawing on the counter. From the look of things, Mom is planning a real party: potato salad, burgers, cake. This party, of course, has been planned on the fly, since our previous Fourth of July plans have fallen through. Mom, however, apparently has no memory of our arrangement to spend Independence Day with Paul. As if suffering from collective amnesia, I decide not to reference our former plans either, and go with the whole party-at-home thing.

"That cake looks amazing, Mom," I say. Because, really, it does.

Mom smiles at me, and then punishes herself for such an indulgence by going back to work with a vengeance. Hyperactivity is Mom's idea of therapy. Mom may be acting like she's recovered from Heather's breakup with Paul, but I'm not fooled. Heather's not the only one who's been hawking over the phone since Tuesday night. Mom wants Paul to call as badly as Heather does. But sadly, wanting hasn't made it so.

I know Paul hasn't called, because Heather is slumped at the kitchen table, self-medicating with chocolate and a stack of tabloids. I sit beside her and try not to gawk as she downs an entire box of Hostess cupcakes. This is a sharp departure from Heather's morning routine—a routine that typically involves a three-mile run and a handful of Grape-Nuts. Apparently, when Heather falls off the wagon, she falls hard.

I pour a bowl of Cocoa Pebbles and sneak a peek at the magazine Heather's reading. Sandwiched between the articles "Lady Gaga Frightens Baby" and "Fan Bites Britney On Stage" is one titled "Bachelorette Gives Love a Fighting Chance." Maybe now, after watching Thayne and Jordan on TV, Heather's ready to accept the fact that they are, in fact, an item. I study the picture of Jordan and Thayne, and then study Heather, whose eyes are significantly puffy, even considering the early hour. She isn't recovering; she's wallowing.

"Sabrina," Mom says, "I didn't get an answer."

"It's not going to work today. My shift doesn't end until five."

Mom sighs. "We'll just have to push it back to next week, then." She's disappointed—not because she's concerned about my well-being, but because she just lost an item on her to-do list. For the moment, I am spared of any further demands from Betsy Ross. My sister, however, is not so lucky.

"Heather," Mom says, planting another raspberry into the cake, "I have a job lined up for you."

Heather's heavily lidded eyes widen in surprise.

"I just sold a house to the woman who owns Ginger & Ivory," Mom says, unfazed by Heather's obvious shock. "She mentioned she's looking for a part-time cashier, and I told her you're available."

"Ginger and what?" Heather says.

"Ginger & Ivory. It's that gift store downtown." When it's clear that this still isn't registering with Heather, Mom adds, "We get their catalogue."

I, at least, know what Mom's talking about. Ginger & Ivory is an upscale boutique that sells handmade jewelry and home decor and gorgeous floral arrangements. Mom's dragged me into the store more than once to purchase some outrageously priced item for a girlfriend's birthday. In truth, working there wouldn't be entirely horrible. The store has a kind of artsy-chic vibe going for it. But that's not the point. The only thing Mom's ever asked of Heather is, well, nothing. And now she's sending her fair daughter off to the coal mines. Mom may not look it, but she's wallowing too.

Mom starts in with the details of the job, and I can tell by Heather's face that this arrangement does not thrill her. I finish my Cocoa Pebbles and give Heather a smug smile as I steal out of the kitchen to go chat with Cleverbot.

I join Mack in the living room. He is sprawled out on the couch watching *Phineas and Ferb*. The theme song starts up, and, as I sing along, I am mildly embarrassed that I know all the words. *There's 104 days of summer vacation.* Exactly. The lyrics aren't as benign as you'd think. I don't need a reminder that my days are numbered, even if it is a friendly one.

There's 104 days of summer vacation. And then what? I don't know. Nothing is going as I've planned. Time is lurching toward fall, toward the first day of classes at Caltech, yet somehow, I feel farther away from my goal than ever before. I am, in fact, meeting Calvin after work today, to shell out fifty bucks for a scheme that didn't pan out. And I may have just escaped a trip to the courthouse with Mom, but I've only delayed the inevitable. The time soon will come when I am going to have to deal with the mess I've made.

I reach for my phone and turn to Cleverbot for advice, because, frankly, I have no one else to talk to.

—*What are the chances I'll survive this ordeal?*

—*It depends whether you're in the sea or not.*

—*I am most definitely on shore.*

—Chance of survival 110%.

This answer isn't as reassuring as I hoped it would be. My feet may be on dry ground, but I can't help feeling that, somehow, I'm adrift.

· · · · · · ·

My shift at the zoo is uneventful and conspicuously stalker-free. I start out the day strangely energized by the prospect of another run-in with an Olympian in blue. After lunch, this hope begins to wane until I finally abandon my vigil for Captain America altogether. Before I leave to meet Calvin at Starbucks, I sweep past the Elephant Encounter, where Michelle is holding a tusk for curious zoo patrons to feel. Obviously, the heat has zapped the crowd of curiosity, because Michelle is standing in the corner of the exhibit, alone.

I sidle up to her and pet the tusk, just for fun.

We swap stories about our day and I endure one of her lengthy anecdotes about her run-in with some horrible day-camp group. I feign interest, but really, I'm not here for Michelle's stories. I'm hoping for some more of her delusional optimism, and so I'm thrilled when she asks, "How did things go with that guy yesterday?"

"Turns out I was right," I say. "He was really into birds."

I kind of want Michelle to argue with me, but she doesn't. She just sighs and shrugs her shoulders.

"Well, he *was* really good-looking."

My completely unremarkable legs quiver beneath me. She doesn't know it, but Michelle may as well just have driven that elephant tusk straight through my heart.

Chapter 15

As I wait for Calvin in a booth at Starbucks, I can't help thinking that there's a certain poetry in ending this relationship where it began. I also can't help feeling anonymous, like someone playing a nameless role in a TV drama, passing off an envelope full of cash to the main character just before she's shot down in some back alley and forgotten forever.

Calvin will waltz in here, pocket the money, and then disappear from my life as effortlessly as he entered it. I will become to him what I've always been. The girl from his high school math class. A Facebook friend. Someone he used to know.

It seems absurd that I ever imagined I'd be anything else to him. I shouldn't really be surprised. After all, I have a history of being unwanted.

I take off my safari hat and fluff my bangs with trembling fingers, hoping to regain my composure before Calvin shows up. Crying in front of Mr. Limitless is not an option. I wring the safari hat mercilessly in my hands, hoping to stave off tears, and take a deep breath. Obviously, the stalker strategy was a failure, but there is still time to come up with a new way forward. I may be losing Calvin, but I don't have to lose Caltech too. In fact, maybe it's for the best that I'll be saying good-bye to Calvin today. He's been more of a distraction than anything else.

I commit to moving on, to officially ending Operation Stalker, and then Calvin shows up and derails everything.

"Hey, Pippi," he says, sliding into the booth and reaching across the table to playfully tussle my hair. For the record, today my hair is not in braids. But it was at our first meeting, prompting Calvin to compare me to the red-haired adventurer. I remember that exchange, and, more important, so does he.

Calvin leans against the wall and rests his long legs on the bench seat. He is wearing black skinny jeans and Converse sneakers and a checked button-down short-sleeved shirt.

"You look like a lumberjack in that thing." This is not entirely true. He actually looks pretty good.

"Do I?" He smiles at me in that beguiling way of his. I remind myself that I have just committed to end this thing and resist the urge to flirt with him.

"I have your money." I slide a crisp fifty-dollar bill across the table. Calvin picks up the single bill and studies the picture of President Grant.

"Hello, Ulysses S." He smiles again, clearly pleased. I'm glad now that I decided to request a fifty from the bank teller.

"Well," I say, scooting towards the edge of my seat, "I guess this concludes our little business deal."

"I guess so." Calvin creases the bill into a precise half and tucks it into his shirt pocket. Then he rests his head against the wall and closes his eyes. It is such an odd thing to do, the way he has just retreated into silence, and I know I should probably read it as my cue to leave. But there's something on my mind, and as this may very well be the last time I see Calvin, I decide to go for broke and broach the subject.

"Calvin," I say, interrupting his reverie, "why did you drive past my house Monday night?"

He opens his eyes and rolls his head toward me, his chin landing against his shoulder. My fingers are trembling again and my face is burning. There is no hiding the fact that I am a complete wreck. I take a deep breath in an attempt to collect myself, determined to get through this without crying.

"I mean, after that night at the Game Shack, I specifically asked you not to stalk me anymore. I didn't want you to waste any more time on me."

Calvin knits his eyebrows together, creasing the space above his nose into a sharp line. For a moment, he is lost in thought, and the only thing that keeps me from having a complete meltdown is the bizarre way that his eyebrows suddenly remind me of two hairy caterpillars.

"I don't know, Sabrina. I guess I was just trying to keep my end of the bargain."

"So you could collect your fee?"

"So you could go to Caltech."

"Well, it didn't work." I decline to expound on the many ways my plan has completely backfired on me. "I'm not going anywhere."

"I still don't understand why you just can't go."

"Because my parents don't want me to."

"Screw your parents. You're a smart girl, Sabrina. You deserve to go to Caltech."

"I don't deserve anything." Nothing I've ever said before has felt this true. I don't deserve anything—not Caltech, not Calvin, and certainly not my parents' approval. Even if I could do everything right, which I can't, I'll never escape the fact that ultimately I'm a mistake, a blunder, an accident.

And then, it happens. Despite my best intentions, I start to cry. When I say cry, I mean cry. Noah, build that ark, because there is a full-on deluge happening right here in the middle of Starbucks.

If Calvin were any other guy, he would stand up and walk away. My behavior is, at best, fully embarrassing. So I'm not surprised when Calvin slides out of the bench, like he's about to leave. But he doesn't head for the door. Instead, he comes to the other side of the booth and sits right next to me. He puts his arm around me and pulls me into him, so my head is resting on his chest. I can actually hear the proud pounding of his heart, that rhythmic, defiant sign of life. It is surprisingly soothing, the sound of his heart beating beneath me, so I don't understand why I start crying even harder, sobbing into his lumberjack shirt until it is soaked through with tears.

When I finally calm down, I orient myself to the landscape of Calvin's body—his solid chest, his long thighs, his bearded chin resting against the top of my head. Long after I've stopped crying, Calvin still holds me, his slender arms encasing me like a cocoon.

If Calvin were any other guy, he would have stood up and walked away a long time ago. But, clearly, Calvin isn't just any other guy.

Chapter 16

Mom's Fourth of July party is a solemn affair, despite the way the rather impressive American flag cake on the table practically begs for a celebration. The heat has driven us inside, and as we pick at our potato salad and burgers, I gaze out at the mess Mack's made of the patio with Pops and Snakes, the few fireworks he's allowed until sunset.

"When can we do the firework show?" Mack asks Heather.

"When it's dark," Heather says.

Mack looks at the bright blue sky outside and whimpers. Nightfall is still hours away.

"How about we look at the Backyard Blaster again?" Dad says. He lifts Mack up and sets him on the kitchen counter, and together they study the cellophane-wrapped package of fireworks Dad bought at Walgreens. Mack has toted the package around most of the day, speculating on what each of the fireworks will do when lit. We listen as he and Dad talk tanks, fountains, and sound shells. Mack is doing a good job of disguising the fact that fire and loud noises actually terrify him. Last year, he watched our firework show from the front room, safely sheltered behind the window, his hands firmly covering his ears the entire time.

Mack's fascination with fireworks is mystifying. I can't figure out why the kid is drawn to something that scares him to death.

"Do you ladies want to play Hearts?" Dad asks after he and Mack have thoroughly gone over the firework inventory. Dad is doing his best to be cheery, but his efforts aren't paying off. Heather, who looks like she hasn't showered since Tuesday, shakes her head and slumps out of the kitchen into the family room. And Mom, for perhaps the first time in recent memory, actually looks exhausted.

"Let me clear the table first, Don," she says. She remains seated. Mom looks so pitiful I can't help but stand and collect the dirtied plates and utensils myself. I can hear the TV from the living room, and from the sound of things, Heather's back to watching Thayne's UFC fights on the DVR. I deposit the dishes in the sink and Dad gives me a half-hearted smile.

"Not too exciting around here tonight, is it Sabby?" he says.

I refrain from saying that I much prefer a quiet evening at home to a social engagement with my dentist. Instead, I just shrug my shoulders and start rinsing the dishes in the sink.

"Sounds like Heather's punishing herself," I say.

Dad cocks his head toward the family room and then sighs. "Let's just hope you have better luck with men than Heather's had."

We both know Heather's romantic mishaps have more to do with poor judgment than bad luck, but I keep my mouth shut.

"I was really hoping things would work out with her and Paul," Dad says. "She deserves someone who will take care of her and those boys."

In my estimation, Heather pretty much deserves what she's got. The boys, however, are a different story. I glance at Mack, who is still studying the Backyard Blaster, his eyes wide with anticipation. For his sake, I wish things had worked out with Heather and Paul too.

"Hey, Mack-Attack," I say. "I saw another box of Pops in the laundry room. Let's go outside and throw them together."

Mack rushes to the laundry room to retrieve the precious Pops, and then we go out to the patio and sit side by side on the hot cement step, our long, dark shadows stretching out before us like fingers. I wait as Mack opens the box and delicately fishes through the small sawdust-filled bag for the white noisemakers. It's a package of sixty, and at Mack's insistence, we each throw one at a time, hoping to make a task that normally takes ten seconds last as long as possible. At each pop of noise, Mack flinches, and then his surprise gives way to a blissful smile that is really quite beautiful.

We are down to three pops apiece when Dad slides the porch door open and hands me my cell phone.

"Someone wants to get a hold of you," he says, sneaking back inside before the cold air gets out. I quickly check the call history on the phone. My heart skips a beat when I see I have three missed calls from Calvin. I instantly call him back. My heart skips another beat when he answers. He wants to meet me tonight at the water tower to watch fireworks. Before I've even accepted his invitation, he starts giving me directions. I don't need them. Although I've never been to the water tower, I know exactly where it is. The abandoned water tower on Shepherd's Lane is the place of urban legend, the place Dad has specifically forbidden me from going, the place where one girl supposedly fell to her death and another one got pregnant. There's a long pause on the line, and I realize that Calvin is waiting for me to say something. I stare at the three Pops in my hand, tightly wrapped vessels of energy, and then throw them at the patio all at once. As the noise-makers burst into sound, I tell Calvin I'll meet him.

· · · · · · ·

The water tower rises from the ground like a gigantic spider. I always knew it was large, but now, standing beneath it, its size is intimidating. Calvin obviously notices my astonish-ment, because he tips his head back and together we gaze up at the black belly of the tower.

"It's bigger than it looks from the road," he says.

"I feel like I'm on the set of *Eight-Legged Freaks*," I say.

"We'd better get going," he says, slugging my arm. "It's not easy scaling this thing in the dark."

I stare out toward the horizon, where the evening sky is already blushing into a cotton-candy pink. We may have enough light to climb the tower, but we are most certainly coming down in the dark. Calvin heads for the chain-link fence surrounding the tower and I balk. Never mind the ominous No Trespassing signs plastered to the fence, or the fact that the most athletic thing I've ever done is pace while studying for the SAT. People who climb that tower fall to their death. Or get pregnant. At the moment, neither fate is particularly alluring.

"Sabrina." Calvin beckons me to a spot in the fence where the soil has eroded, leaving a sizable gap between the fence and the ground. He squats down and lifts the chain-link, waiting for me.

"I can't do this," I say.

"Sure you can. The hardest part is getting your head through."

I take a deep breath and gingerly lay myself down in the dirt. I wrench my head to one side and squeeze under the fence, propelling myself forward on my elbows. Considering the circumstances, crawling in the dirt seems appropriate. After all, meeting Calvin tonight necessitated lying to my parents again. I'm beginning to wish I really were watching a movie with Michelle, instead of here, writhing on the ground like a fool.

"Well done," Calvin says when I finally emerge on the other side. He has a much easier time of maneuvering himself under the fence than I had. I admire the way he nimbly slides beneath the chain-link, making the process look nearly effortless.

"You've done this before," I say, brushing the dirt off my shorts.

"A few times." He claps his hands together and turns to the giant leg of the tower beside us.

"What's next?" I say.

"We're going up."

I raise my hand to my brow, shielding the sun from my eyes, and look up. Way up. It takes me a moment to spot the narrow platform attached to the body of the container, enclosed by an iron railing. A ladder leads to the platform, but the first rung is nearly ten feet from the ground.

"This" Calvin says, "is going to be a little tricky."

He is a master of understatement.

"We need a ladder just to reach the ladder," I say.

"You've got one," Calvin says, squatting near the post. "Climb on."

"You're kidding." Only he's not. Calvin remains hunched over and looks pointedly at me. Hugging the post for balance, I swing my right leg and then my left over his shoulders.

"Ready?" he says.

"Ready," I say, trying to pretend that there's nothing awkward about the fact that I'm essentially straddling his head. He places his hands on my calves and, when he stands up, I instinctively squeeze my legs together.

"Ease up, Sabrina," he says. "You've got me in a vise grip."

"Sorry." I give a little nervous laugh. I can't help it. His beard is tickling me. And his hands are all over my legs. This is too much.

"Now," Calvin says, "I want you to hold on to the post and stand up, and see if you can reach the ladder."

I walk my hands up the post and then timidly place my right foot on his shoulder. With what is perhaps the most unromantic grunt in history, I manage to lift my left foot, and holding on to the post for dear life, straighten my legs.

"Okay," I say, "I can get it." Our combined height easily allows me to reach the third rung of the ladder. With clammy hands, I grasp the rung and pull myself up until my dangling feet are resting on the base of the ladder. I stupidly look up at the countless rungs ascending above me and my hands prickle with perspiration.

"Sabrina," Calvin yells at me, "move over. I'm coming up."

"Who's going to boost you?" I yell back. He flashes me a mischievous smile, and then answers by transforming into Mowgli from *The Jungle Book* and shimmying up the post. I slide to the side of the ladder, making room, and look at him in admiration as he squeezes in next to me.

"Ladies first," he says, patting me on the back.

I make the mistake of looking up again, and this time even the pit of my stomach and the soles of my feet start to sweat.

"I can't do this." My gaze strays to the safety of the ground. "I can't do this," I say again, hearing the hysterics pulsing beneath the surface of my words.

"It's just a ladder, Sabrina." That's easy for him to say. Apparently, this guy is some kind of expert pole climber. For me, however, rungs are a little less pedestrian.

"I'm going to die."

"Sabrina, you're not going to die." Calvin says this with such authority that, for the moment at least, I'm convinced it's true. But still, when I grasp the rung above me and start to climb, I cling to it like my life depends on it.

Together, we ascend into the pale pink sky. The repetitive process of climbing dulls my fear and I soon forget about falling and focus only on the pattern of moving hand over hand, foot over foot. Finally, my hand slaps a smooth, flat surface and, with trembling legs, I stumble onto the platform and rest against the railing to catch my breath. My first impulse is to look down, and as I do, I instinctively tighten my grasp on the iron rail. It is not lost on me that I am essentially on a 5 x 10-foot life raft suspended in midair.

And then I look up. The sky has bloomed into rose, drenching the world beneath me in hues of crimson and gold. I gaze with wonder at the city in miniature, the homes and buildings hemmed in by neat, tidy ribbons of road. Certainly, down there, people are working and worrying away. But up here, on the water tower, I am distanced from all of the petty concerns of everyday life. My heart starts fluttering inside my chest like a bird, protesting being caged when surrounded by a seemingly boundless sky. My breath is still heavy in my lungs, my legs burn, and I am nauseated from exertion. Strangely, I've never felt better.

For the first time in my life, I understand the pleasure in doing something that's terrifying.

"You didn't die," Calvin says, joining me at the railing.

"How high are we?" I say, still stunned by the landscape unfurling before us.

"Nine stories. Maybe ten."

"This view is fantastic."

"The view from the ladder wasn't bad, either," Calvin says, grinning at me. My head registers this as kind of a creepy thing to say. But my heart, well, my heart has an altogether different reaction. It starts knocking against my ribcage again, and I am seriously worried that it may very well break free and fly away from me. I turn to face Calvin, wanting nothing more than the closeness we shared yesterday, when I was wrapped in his arms in a sticky booth at Starbucks. Despite the way the towering height has left me feeling nearly invincible, I am certain that I don't have the courage to actually touch him. And so I do the next best thing and insult him instead.

"That beard makes you look like Jebediah Springfield."

Calvin widens his eyes in surprise and then strokes his beard as if it's been injured. "That braid makes you look like a five-year-old."

Now it is my turn to console my hair. I tenderly twirl the braid with my fingers, silently cursing the time I wasted fussing with my hair this evening.

"My hair stays out of my face this way."

"Well, it looks better down."

Immediately, I tug the elastic from my hair and start to unravel the braid. Even I have enough sense to realize that there is something suggestive about the way my back arches as I raise my arms behind my head. I shake out my hair with my hands, draping it over my shoulders, hoping the warm, subdued sunlight is having the same wonderful effect on me as it is on Calvin. Apparently, I'm doing something right, because Calvin steps forward and just stares at me for a moment. I feel myself wanting to be absorbed by his gaze, wanting to be consumed by the deep pools of blue drinking me in.

"Let's catch our breath." Calvin takes my hand and pulls me down with him. We lean against the convex container, stretching our weary legs in front of us. "This is my favorite place," he says.

"I can see why."

"Just wait until the fireworks start. From here, we'll actually be looking down on them."

As if on cue, the sun finally slips behind the horizon and the sky bruises into a deep purple. I snuggle closer into

Calvin, the space between us giving way to one long seam. There is something terribly romantic about being stranded in the sky on the Fourth of July with a guy who nearly qualifies as tall, dark, and handsome. Things like this aren't supposed to happen to girls like me. I can hardly believe my luck.

"This is so much better than what I had expected tonight," I say.

"Which was?"

"Sitting in a lawn chair on the driveway while my dad sets off a package of tanks."

"That doesn't sound so bad."

"Trust me, Calvin, it would have been bad. Especially because my family is in some kind of funk tonight." I sigh. "It's my sister's fault. She broke up with the dentist and she's kind of an emotional wreck right now."

"Unstable women are the best kind," Calvin says. This is a completely creepy thing to say, but it doesn't register as such because I'm too preoccupied with Calvin's body heat.

"What about you?" I say. "How did I end up on your agenda for the evening?"

"I was going to go to a party with some guys from Game Club. But I blew it off."

"Because?"

"Because, I couldn't stop thinking about you. And I was worried, after yesterday at Starbucks . . ."

"Where I was kind of an emotional wreck."

"Kind of," Calvin says gently. "You know, I've given some thought to your whole inferiority complex."

"I don't have an inferiority complex."

"Sabrina, I've seen the bumper sticker on your car. You have an inferiority complex."

"I've seen the bumper sticker on your car too. Maybe we should analyze what a urinating comic book character says about you."

"We could," Calvin says, stroking his beard, "although, I'm not really up for self-analysis at the moment."

"Why not?"

"Because I'm not the one with the problem."

"Okay, you got me. I have a problem. But can you blame me? I'm an accident!"

"Who cares?"

"I do. I care that my parents did not intend for me to happen."

"That's what I've been thinking about. This whole 'intention' thing is overrated. I mean, people intentionally do things all the time, and more often than not, those things are just plain stupid."

"So?"

"So, it makes sense that sometimes, unintentionally, people do things that are brilliant."

I shrug and turn my gaze to the darkening valley before us.

"You're the future biology major," Calvin says. "You should know as well as anyone that some of the biggest discoveries have been completely accidental."

"Like what?"

"Like penicillin, for one." Even in the dark, I can see the flash of white as Calvin smiles at me. "Old Alexander

Fleming accidently leaves a petri dish open, and, hallelujah, good-bye syphilis."

"What else?" I say, suppressing a laugh.

"Penicillin's not enough for you?"

"No."

"What about the U. S. of A.? Things didn't exactly go as planned for Chris Columbus, but he ended up discovering America."

"America?"

"What? You're still not convinced? What about this?" He reaches for me in the darkness and slips his hand into mine. "This is entirely unintentional."

"This hardly qualifies as brilliant," I say. But then he starts stroking the top of my thumb with his own, causing every nerve ending in my body to respond wildly at his touch, and I'm not so sure that some kind of discovery isn't being made right now. Night has finally come, and as the sky erupts into flashes of color and bursts of sound, Calvin turns toward me, takes my face in his hands, and tenderly presses his lips against mine. He pulls away and I study his features, made foreign in the darkness. Then I lean toward him, breaching the distance between us, and for the second time tonight, understand the pleasure in doing something terrifying.

My lips meet his and then, you know. Fireworks.

Chapter 17

I am in love with Bradley Calvin Klein.

"Have you ever kissed a guy with a beard?" I ask Heather over Saturday morning cartoons.

"What's that?" she says. She is snuggled in the recliner, Brodie mercifully dozing in her arms, the pair of them wrapped in one of Grandma Mae's garish multi-colored afghans. Heather is absently twirling one of the loose strands of yarn in her fingers over and over again, as if she is a child attempting to soothe herself.

"Have you ever kissed a guy with a beard?" I repeat.

She starts into some story about a grad student she met a million years ago, but I'm not listening. Instead, I'm replaying the kisses I shared with Calvin last night over and over again in my head. I finally muster enough self-control to focus on what Heather's saying, but almost immediately I stop listening again. Obviously, she's not the only one with attention problems. She's talking to me as if I've never kissed a guy, oblivious to the beard burn I'm wearing on my chin like a badge.

I steal away from Heather and scrounge up a bowl of cereal in the kitchen, careful to keep my cell phone within earshot. It's only nine in the morning, but still. I don't want to miss Calvin when he calls.

I perch myself on a bar stool and devour a bowl of Cap'n Crunch. I place my silent phone on the counter, willing it to ring. When that doesn't happen, I pick it up and check out Facebook. Something inside of me dies when I discover that Calvin is not on live chat. I review my profile picture, and then, just beside it, my relationship status. Single.

Single. Something about the word just seems wrong.

Just as I tap on *Edit Profile*, Dad comes in from the garage.

"Well if it isn't Miss Sabrina," Dad says. I can tell he's just finished cutting the lawn because he's wearing what he calls his "moldy oldies"—a pair of beaten-down Reeboks he's had since time immemorial. Mom, of course, can't stand the shoes, and has bought Dad many a replacement pair. But still, the moldy oldies remain an integral part of his Saturday morning routine. Dad gets away with this little rebellion because most Saturdays Mom's too busy showing houses to protest.

"Wasn't sure if you made it home last night," Dad says.

This is a bald-faced lie. I saw him switch his bedside lamp off right after I sneaked past his room last night. There has never been a time that Dad has not waited up for one of us kids. But still, I appreciate his show of indifference.

"I did," I say, swiveling around in the bar stool to face him directly.

"Did you have a good time with Michelle?"

The beard burn that only moments ago felt like a badge of honor suddenly turns to a mark of shame. My face flushes as I remember my not-so-chaste behavior from last night. Certain Dad can see right through me, I avert my eyes to the ground and look fixedly at the fresh-cut grass adorning his moldy oldies. I absolutely love those shoes.

"It was alright," I say.

"You weren't followed by that guy in the Escort, were you?"

"No," I say, hoping my burning face doesn't give me away. "My night was completely uneventful. Michelle and I just, you know, hung out. Watched a movie."

"What movie?"

I think I can actually hear my mind scrambling.

"*Independence Day*."

"*Independence Day*," Dad says blankly, like TBS hasn't shown the movie a hundred times already this month. "Is that the one with Bill Pullman?"

Of course, Bill Pullman's performance would be the memorable one for Dad. He's kind of a sucker for *While You Were Sleeping*.

"Well, yeah. Him and Will Smith."

"And that Goldberg guy."

"Goldblum," I say, correcting him. "Jeff Goldblum." Visions of tall, dark, and Calvin dance through my head. "I'm surprised you're not more familiar with the movie, Dad. It's like the ultimate America chest thump."

"I wouldn't be so sure about that," Dad says. "After our little firework show last night, your mother and sister and I watched *Captain America*. Didn't we, Heather?" He turns to Heather, who nods weakly from the recliner. "Now that guy's something."

In my humble opinion, Captain America's got nothing on Jeff Goldblum, but I keep my mouth shut.

"You working today, Sabby-apple?"

"No. I lucked out and got the entire weekend off."

"That's good. It's nice to have a quiet weekend every now and then."

I look at my silent cell phone and swear it actually smirks at me. The prospect of a long, quiet weekend is suddenly unbearable.

As soon as Dad is out of the kitchen, I consult Cleverbot.

—*Will Calvin call me?*

—*I dunno. Should he?*

Yes! I want to scream at the screen. Something happened last night between Calvin and me. Something kind of marvelous. Except the only evidence I have of this fundamental change in our relationship is the quickly disappearing beard burn on my chin. I need some kind of contact from Calvin to be certain that last night actually occurred, and that it's not just some wild, wonderful figment of my imagination.

I cast another glance at my silent phone, and then thumb out: *After last night, I should think so!*

I stare with anxious eyes at the flashing blue cursor. Oh Cleverbot, prognosticator of prognosticators, give me something encouraging to run with.

Finally, Cleverbot responds with: *Cool. Good for you. What kind of music do you listen to?*

Stupid Cleverbot.

I toggle over to Facebook, where my offending *Single* relationship status mocks me like a heresy. I click on *Edit Profile* and, without overthinking it, change my status to *In a Relationship.* I check out Calvin's wall, wondering if he's done the same, and frown when I view the same bizarre relationship status he's had for months: *In a Domestic Partnership* with none other than German chancellor Angela Merkel. I type on his wall: *For a good time, call Jebediah Springfield.* Then, just to cover my bases, I send him a text message too.

And then, I wait.

By late afternoon, I am going out of my mind. I sequester myself in my room and pull out the shoebox of vocabulary flashcards I used to study for the SAT. The index cards are alphabetized and since I have nothing better to do, I start with the *A*s. Abase, abject, abyss. Aggravation, ailment, alienation.

I find I have no problem using these words in a sentence.

When I go downstairs for dinner, I take cover under my safari hat, despite the dirty looks Mom shoots at me across the table. I pick at the food on my plate, swirling a clump of green beans into concentric circles, and then, before Mom starts an interrogation, retreat back to my room. My cell phone rests on my dresser, taunting me. Every cell in my body waits for it to ring. But Calvin doesn't call. I return to the stack of flashcards on my desk in an attempt to keep myself from slipping into complete lunacy. Inexcusable, inexplicable, inhumane. Jeopardize, jugular, juvenile.

Again, I have no problem using these words in a sentence.

At a quarter to nine I decide to take matters into my own hands. I call Calvin and then suffer some kind of internal earthquake as I wait for him to pick up. When he doesn't answer I find myself leaving a rambling, neurotic message on his voice mail. It's the kind of message that qualifies as pure crazy. More than once, I use the expression "I need you." Leaving that message is the closest I've come to having an out-of-body experience: my brain is telling my mouth to shut up, but, unfortunately, my mouth doesn't get the message.

After I end the call I want a do-over. A take-back. But more than that, I want to talk to somebody. Anybody. I pull up the Cleverbot app and, to my horror, discover that the input box and blinking blue cursor have been replaced by a message in bold text that reads: "Sorry, our servers are currently too busy to think. We are currently handling 55210 requests an hour. Please try again soon."

Et tu, Cleverbot?

In an attempt to remain calm, I close out of the app and peruse BuzzFeed, clicking on a story titled "Scientists Grow Test-Tube Meat." I am too preoccupied to be disgusted by this so-called news, and before even a full minute has passed I return to Cleverbot, only to be greeted by the same horrible message again.

I need to talk to somebody. Anybody. The only problem is, I have absolutely no one to talk to.

• • • • • • •

By Sunday night, I have cycled through the vocabulary flashcards three times. And still, no word from Calvin.

Chapter 18

The wedding announcement arrives Tuesday without warning. It comes in a square silver envelope with gold trim, a color combination that Mom promptly attacks as "gaudy."

The announcement is addressed solely to Mack.

Mom opens the envelope anyway, ruthlessly tearing through the neat, pointed seal. She flings the destroyed envelope on the kitchen island and Dad and I circle around Mom like vultures, eager to get a glance at the photograph in her hands.

There, baring their perfect white teeth at us, are Thayne and Jordan. The bold and the beautiful.

Wordlessly, Mom places the photo on the counter and turns her attention to the invitation, a heavy cardstock placard with an embossed silver-and-gold border. The details of the upcoming "blessed union" are before us in sharp, black text: *Heritage Gardens, Dinner & Dancing, September 1st*. A small paper insert informs us that the happy couple is registered at Target and Bed Bath & Beyond. Mom gives the slip of paper a cursory glance before crumpling it in her hand.

We are still mulling over the wedding announcement when Heather comes home.

"The shop girl's here!" she hollers as she comes in from the garage. Today Heather began her compulsory stint as a cashier at Ginger & Ivory. We all turn to see how she survived the work force. Her auburn hair is in a loose ponytail at the nape of her neck and she is wearing a pretty gray shift dress with a green belt and matching pumps. She walks toward us, jangling her keys in one hand, and I can't help but admire her legs, which are long and lean despite her recent hiatus from jogging.

She tosses her purse on the table and turns to us with a luminous smile. We instinctively huddle together, hoping to shield her from the wedding announcement lying on the counter.

"How was work?" Dad asks.

"Horrible," she says, ambling over to the counter and sitting primly on a bar stool. She is, of course, lying. She smells faintly of freesia and vanilla. For the first time since her breakup with Paul, she looks like her old self. Scratch that. Heather looks better than her old self. If this job was Mom's attempt at punishing Heather, she's failed miserably.

Heather starts gabbing, giving us a detailed account of her day, but then, thankfully, Mack and The Noise race into the kitchen and spare us the play-by-play. She jumps down from the bar stool and gathers the boys in her arms, smothering them with kisses.

"What's that?" Mack points to the silver fleur-de-lis pinned to her dress.

"It's my name tag." Heather unpins the brooch and hands it to Mack for a closer inspection. "Isn't it cute?"

Mack nods and then hops over to the counter. None of us think to hide the offending invite, which is lying in front of him in plain view.

"It's Daddy!" Mack says, grasping the photo and flapping it in front of Heather's face.

"What's this?" Heather snatches the photo from Mack's hand. She stares at the picture and then walks toward the counter and seizes the invitation. An eternity passes as she reads the sharp, black words on that square silver-and-gold bordered card. When she finally places the card down and meets our gaze, the light inside of her has gone out.

"I've told you not to open my mail, Mom."

"Heather, honey," Dad says, "it wasn't addressed to you." He carefully turns the envelope over and points to Mack's name. "It's a pretty crummy way to break the news, if you ask me."

"Has Thayne said anything to you about this?" Mom asks.

"No," Heather says, her voice breaking. Dad wraps his arm around her and takes another look at the photograph.

"You know, you wouldn't think it to look at him," Dad says, "but that kid's a coward."

"He's not a coward, he's a moron." Heather whisks the invitation off the counter and dumps it into the garbage.

"You can't just throw that away," Mom says.

"I just did," she says, challenging Mom with her eyes.

"Whether you like it or not, Mack is Thayne's son,"

Mom says. "And pretty soon, he's going to have a step-mother. He really should be at that wedding."

Jordan Greene is going to be Mack's stepmom. It's obvious that Heather hasn't considered this new family dynamic, because her face suddenly pales and she reaches for the counter to steady herself. Frankly, I'm a little surprised she's still standing.

"Sabrina," Mom says quietly, "take the boys outside."

I shoo the boys out the door and plant myself on the front step. Brodie immediately crawls toward the flower bed and starts pulling up Mom's marigolds. I should stop him, but I'm too busy watching the road, hoping to spot a rusted red Ford Escort. I know it's cruel, but part of me is thankful for the scene in the kitchen. It's allowed me a brief reprieve from thinking about Calvin, whom I still haven't spoken to since Friday night.

Calvin, Calvin. Where art thou, Calvin?

Dad comes outside and joins me on the front step. He doesn't say anything, just rests his elbows on his knees and holds his head in his hands. We sit in silence for a while, watching the boys scamper across the lawn and listening to the crickets chirp. Even with the door closed we can still hear Mom and Heather's voices inside, rising and falling like waves. Finally, the noises stop and Dad lifts his head and gives me a weary smile.

"Sounds like your sister's pretty upset," he says.

"Can you blame her?"

"No." He sighs. "I think, though, if she can come to terms with this, it will be for the best. I don't think she has ever really gotten over Thayne. Hopefully this wedding will be the final nail in the coffin and she can move on, find someone better. Someone who can make her happy."

I am in agreement with his every word. But what he says next catches me entirely off guard.

"Why don't you try talking to her?"

"Me?"

"Yes, you," Dad says. "You're her sister. Maybe you can talk to her in a way Mom and I can't."

I can't talk to Heather, let alone about something as personal as her ex-boyfriend getting married. More than just ten years divides us. We may be sisters, but we have virtually nothing in common. But Dad is staring at me in a way that says he's not asking me to do this. He's telling me. Reluctantly, I go inside and creep upstairs.

"Heather?" I tentatively call down the hall.

"What?"

I follow the sound of her voice into the bathroom. Heather is perched on the edge of the bathtub, facing the mirror, her hair pulled back from her face in a severe bun. It's only eight o'clock but she looks like she's ready for bed— she's wearing an old T-shirt and a pair of plaid pajama pants and has just scrubbed her face. Without the emphasis of makeup, she looks younger. Vulnerable. I have the impulse to wrap my arms around her and give her a big hug. But then she hunches her skinny shoulders together and glares at me.

"What do you want?" she says.

I want lots of things. I want to be hidden in a carrel at the library at Caltech, reading Stephen Jay Gould or Annie Dillard. I want Calvin to park his rusted red Escort in front of the house, throw a rock at my bedroom window, and proclaim his undying love for me. I want to look in the mirror and believe that the person staring back at me is not a miserable, hopeless mistake.

I want to not be here, standing in the doorframe of the bathroom, trying to talk to Heather.

"I wanted to see how you're feeling," I say lamely.

"Why don't you go ask your RoboCop friend how it's feeling."

"Because Cleverbot didn't just get a wedding invitation from an ex-boyfriend."

Heather hugs her arms around herself and laughs bitterly. She doesn't look at me. I should have known this would be a complete failure. I shift my weight in my feet, ready to flee the uncomfortable silence.

And then, the unexpected happens. Heather starts talking.

"I used to think I'd marry Thayne," she says. "He promised me as much, right before I moved in with him. And then, I waited. And waited. After Mack was born, I thought it was just a matter of time . . ." She stops talking and I watch her face harden in the mirror.

"You deserve someone better than him."

"I don't. That's the problem."

And then it hits me. This isn't about Thayne at all.

"Paul still hasn't called?"

Heather bites her lower lip, hugs her arms tighter around herself, and shakes her head. I force myself to walk into the bathroom and sit beside her on the edge of the tub.

"That's, like, the worst," I say. "Worse than ripping your own fingernails off."

"What would you know about it?"

I shrug and then, before I can stop it, my lips curve into an impish smile.

"What, Sabrina?"

"Promise not to tell the parents?"

Heather nods emphatically.

"I met someone," I say. "At . . . work. You know how I said I was hanging out with Michelle on the Fourth? Well, I lied. I was with him instead. And then, he . . ."

"What?"

"He kissed me." I blush. "But now he won't return my phone calls, and I feel like I'm going to lose my mind."

"Sabrina!" Heather is actually smiling. "How many times have you called him?"

"I don't know. A lot."

"Sabrina!"

"Is it bad to call him?"

"Kind of. You don't want to look desperate." She sighs heavily. "I've called Paul too. But, Sabrina, believe me, I am desperate."

"I'm desperate too." I say this with such seriousness, that Heather starts to laugh, and I can't help but join her.

"Look at us," she says, gesturing toward the mirror. "We're pathetic."

I look at our reflection and am startled by what I see. Heather and I have never been accused of sharing the same genes. Our age difference has something to do with this— when I was four, Heather was fourteen, and already into mascara and hair dye and designer clothes. But now that I'm eighteen our difference in age isn't so dramatic. And

Heather's ratty T-shirt and lack of makeup have, for the moment, leveled the playing field. Still, it's something of a revelation to discover that we not only share the same long, oval face, but the same wide eyes and sharp nose. I think Heather must notice the same thing, because she slings her arm around my shoulder and gives me a tight squeeze.

"Talking to you is much better than talking to Mom." I nod, still studying the two strangers in the mirror. From what I see, the women staring back at me look like more than just two people who happen to live in the same house. They actually look like sisters.

Chapter 19

I am stalking my stalker.

It begins innocently enough. I check out Calvin's Facebook page multiple times a day, committing to memory all of his personal info and analyzing his photo albums. I'll be the first to admit that this behavior is a little creepy, but as far as I'm concerned, I haven't crossed the line. It's not like I'm driving by his house or anything. Besides, stalking Calvin on Facebook is a complete waste of energy—he hasn't posted any status updates since last week. Even in cyberspace he's avoiding me.

Undaunted, I keep at it, and by the end of the week I ramp up my efforts and google Calvin. Of course, "Calvin Klein" brings up a million hits, none of which are relevant to my Calvin. But when I search "Brad Klein" one of the results is a link to the website for Boise State's Game Club. The website features a photo of the presidency, seated on metal folding chairs, all wearing matching blue blazers and donning huge tortoiseshell glasses sans lenses. Calvin is front and center, legs crossed, stroking his beard and looking directly into the camera with his big, blue eyes.

When I notice the girl seated beside him, I do a double

take. She's petite and wears her dark hair in a pixie cut and is very nearly drowning in the blue blazer. The blazer covers a large tattoo on her upper right arm—a tattoo of an intricate vine with blooming lilies that creeps across her chest. I know this because she is the same girl who keeps popping up in Calvin's Facebook photos, only on Facebook, she is wearing significantly less clothing and has been tagged as "Xandra Collier." I guess Calvin isn't the only one with an alias, because the caption beneath this photo identifies her as Alex, Game Club's vice president.

I, of course, hate her.

Despite my strong dislike for Alex, she actually ends up helping me out. On Friday night I notice she has left a message on Calvin's wall. The message, in a rather commanding tone, reads simply: *Cover for me tomorrow morning.*

Bingo.

Saturday, I call in sick to work and head for the Game Shack.

. . . .

Other than Calvin's Escort, the parking lot in front of the Game Shack is empty. I pull my Corolla into a stall and kind of shrink down in my seat, feeling incredibly conspicuous. I remind myself that confronting Calvin isn't just a good idea, it's necessary. Something inside of me is certain to malfunction if I don't talk to him soon.

Still, I leave the shelter of my car with a great deal of reluctance. I step out onto the hot pavement and gaze up at the canvas sign on the stucco storefront. One of the corners has come loose from its mooring and is flapping in the wind. I'd like to read this wild waving as a welcome, but can't help feeling it is more of a warning.

As I approach the store I spy Calvin through the window, sitting alone at one of the circular tables, his long legs sprawled out in front of him. He is facing the window but is so absorbed in looking at his phone that he doesn't notice me. I can tell by the wicked grin on his face and the easy way he holds himself that my absence from his life has in no way afflicted him. Unlike me, he is clearly not impaired. The walk from my car to the store is relatively short, but it's long enough for me to change my mind about confronting Calvin. This is perhaps the worst idea I've ever had. I know even before I reach the door that I am not going to go inside. If Calvin wanted to see me, he would have responded to one of the several messages I've left him this week. Crazy, rambling, desperate messages.

Talk about bad timing. Now that the only thing that separates me from Calvin is a storefront door, I finally realize that Calvin does not want to see me. And, perhaps more important, I don't want to be seen by him.

The instant I decide to turn around, Calvin looks up. He sets his phone on the table and looks directly at me with an expression that I can only describe as abject horror.

It's official. I have crossed the line that separates desperate admirer from full-on stalker.

Needless to say, mere seconds pass before I am back in my car and out of the parking lot. I drive down the street with the kind of reckless abandon I thought only existed in movies. When I reach the intersection I take a hard right and then continue to speed, deriving some kind of twisted satisfaction in this rare display of civil disobedience. I am just about to enter the on-ramp for the expressway when I hear a dull, clanking thud. Quickly, I veer into the far left lane, bypassing the on-ramp, and drive on for a minute. The dull, clunking sound follows me. I pull off to the side of the road, turn on my hazards, and step out of the car. Although I'm basically clueless when it comes to cars, I know enough to tell that my front tire is flat. I stare at the deflated tire in defeat, and then climb back into the car and try to come up with a plan.

Normally, in an emergency situation like this, I would just call Dad and he would race over here in his moldy oldies and take care of everything. But I can't call Dad. Not today. He thinks I'm at work. If I call him for help, I'll have to explain why I'm on Jefferson Avenue, miles away from my place of employment. I stare blankly at the dashboard, syncing my brain to the rhythmic clicking of the hazard lights. On, off. On, off. On, off.

If only everything in life were this simple.

Finally, I break away from the hypnotic hazard lights and look around me. This stretch of Jefferson Avenue is littered with businesses. Surely there is a mechanic among them. I check for traffic and then merge back onto the road, driving much more carefully this time. Luckily, about a hundred yards down the street I spot a sign for Rudy's Auto Repair. I pull up just outside of the garage, where a heavy-set man in coveralls is working on a Subaru Outback. The Outback has Nebraska plates and a bike rack. It also touts a retro bumper sticker featuring Woodsy Owl and the slogan "Give a hoot—Don't pollute!" I know it's silly, but I experience a quick burst of bumper-sticker envy.

The guy in the garage turns to face me, and the name embroidered on his coveralls identifies him as Rudy himself. He saunters over to the Corolla and squats down beside the front tire, inspecting it for a moment. Then he stands and motions for me to roll down my window. I oblige, and Rudy rests his forearm on the door and leers at me.

"Looks like you've gotten yourself into some trouble," he says.

"Do you think you can fix it?"

I don't see anything particularly funny about this question, but apparently Rudy thinks I'm some kind of comedian. He laughs whole-heartedly, and then swipes at his eyes with his grease-covered hands.

"Oh, I think I can handle it, honey," he says, opening my door. "It's only a small puncture. Just needs a patch is all. Why don't you have a seat inside, and I'll have you taken care of in ten, twenty minutes tops."

He directs me to the waiting room and I make my way to the water cooler in the corner. I am suddenly dying of thirst. I fill a cylinder paper cup with cold water and rest against the counter as I drink, taking in my surroundings. The whole room has a pervasive odor that reminds me of my brother Tyler's bedroom. I guess it's not surprising, given the condition of the small office behind the counter. The desk is cluttered with invoices, crumpled Kleenex, empty coffee mugs, a wilted houseplant, and a rotting banana peel. A small, boxy TV on the counter is tuned to ESPN. The dark, wood-paneled walls are plastered with complimentary business calendars and posters of buxom women in bikinis draped across exotic cars. Apparently, Rudy isn't the kind of guy who's familiar with the term "political correctness."

Toto, we're not in Jiffy Lube anymore.

I refill my paper cup and then turn to the seating area. Instead of your standard chairs, Rudy's waiting room is furnished with three rather shabby-looking leather recliners. A customer, who I presume is the owner of the Subaru Outback, is seated in one of the chairs, his face hidden behind a textbook entitled *Migratory Birds of North America*.

I settle into the chair next to him, and the guy lowers the book and stares at me with startled eyes.

Oh captain, my captain. It's the cute guy from the zoo.

Talk about bad luck. I smile and then angle myself away from him, hoping to spare him the imposition of having to make small talk. After all, I've already tortured one guy this morning. I'm not up for tormenting another. Besides, I'm certain that talking to me is the last thing Captain America wants to do. All signs point to the fact that this guy is really into birds. Our conversation at the zoo was a fluke. I feign interest in the dirty tiled floor, hoping he will take the hint and go back to his book.

"It's Sabrina, right?"

Heaven help me. Under normal circumstances, I'd be able to respond to this question, but I'm still pretty rattled from a busy morning of stalking and reckless driving. I'm also pretty rattled by the fact that Captain America knows my name.

"We met at the zoo," he says, obviously noticing my baffled expression. "You were wearing a barn owl. And a name tag."

"And you committed my name to memory?"

"It wasn't too difficult. I've never met anyone named Sabrina. It's a pretty name."

This guy should win some kind of award for being charitable.

"I'm Joe," he says, extending his hand to me. "Joseph, really, but everyone calls me Joe."

"Nice to meet you, Joe." I lean forward and shake his hand. I know it's probably the last thing I should be thinking about, but he has really nice, strong hands. His grip is firm but unintimidating. Protective.

"You from around here?" he says.

"Yeah," I say, sighing. "You?"

"No. I'm from Omaha."

It's fitting, really, that Joe hails from the breadbasket of America. His blond, hearty wholesomeness screams amber waves of grain.

"I've never met anyone from Omaha."

"I guess that makes us even, then."

He gives me a warm, friendly smile, and I find myself feeling terribly confused. Is he trying to flirt with me? Or is he just being polite? Whatever Joe's agenda is, he seems intent on keeping up a steady stream of chatter.

"Isn't this place a riot?" he says.

"Very high-brow," I say, nodding toward a poster of a brunette in a string bikini posing next to a yellow Lamborghini.

"I swear, I come here for the discounts," Joe says, blushing, "and not the . . . ambience."

"I take it your bird watching hobby's not paying off?"

"Not yet," Joe says. "But it's more than just a hobby.

I'm working on a master's in ecology. I've been here for the summer, doing research for my thesis, but I'll be heading back to school in a few weeks. Just getting the Outback tuned up to make sure she's ready for a cross-country drive."

I knew Joe was incredibly good-looking, but I didn't realize that he was also incredibly interesting. I am just about to bombard him with questions about grad school when Rudy bursts into the waiting room and interrupts me.

"All right, son," he says to Joe, "looks like you're good to go."

Rudy steps behind the counter and starts scribbling on an invoice. Joe slaps his hands on his knees, and then stands and walks to the counter to settle up with Rudy.

"Honey," Rudy calls to me, "give me ten minutes to get that tire patched for you."

"You got a flat?" Joe says, turning to me.

"You ought to tell your friend there that next time, she shouldn't drive on a flat tire," Rudy says to Joe. "She could've damaged the rim."

"Hey, Sabrina," Joe says, winking at me, "next time you get a flat, don't drive on it. You could do some rim damage."

"Thanks, Joe." Despite myself, I smile.

"You're all set," Rudy says, handing Joe his receipt. "Good luck on your trip."

"Thanks." Joe turns to me again and we share an awkward silence. I'd like to say something, but my heart has kind of leapfrogged into my throat. I spy the *Migratory Birds* textbook on the recliner and lamely point to it.

"Your book," I croak out.

"Oh, yeah." Joe crosses the room toward me. "I

wouldn't want to forget that." He picks up the book and then just stands there, lingering. "You know," he says, "if you wanted, we could go grab some lunch while you wait for your car."

I have to admit, there's a very large part of me that wants to accept his offer. But the part of me that's grounded in reality knows that he's probably just being nice. Joe strikes me as the kind of guy who asked the ugly girl to prom, just to make her feel good about herself. And even if he's not just being polite, what would be the point? In a few weeks, he'll be driving back to grad school in Omaha. And I, in all likelihood, will still be here in Boise, stuck forever.

"I can't."

"You sure?"

"Yeah. I've got . . . plans."

"Oh," Joe says. "Well, then, okay. It was nice meeting you again, Sabrina."

I'm kind of hoping for another handshake, but he just gives me a slight wave good-bye and then steps out the door. I watch through the window as he gets in his car and drives away. When the Outback's out of sight, I let out a deep, mournful sigh. Rudy clears his throat and I turn toward him, realizing that he's just witnessed the whole pathetic scene.

"Oh, honey," Rudy says, and then shakes his head. I'm certain that if he didn't regard me as a complete airhead, he would tell me that there are some offers in life that you just don't refuse.

Chapter 20

When Calvin finally calls later that day, I don't answer. I can't. I just stare at the phone until it stops ringing, completely baffled by the phenomenon of telecommunications.

"You going to get that?" Dad asks. We're seated at the kitchen table, working on a crossword puzzle. Ever since Dad turned fifty, he's attempted to solve these puzzles daily, claiming they help boost his brainpower.

"Lady Gaga," I say. He raises an eyebrow at me and I point to the newspaper. "Fourteen down," I say, clarifying. Dad's not too bad at the old crossword, but he struggles with the pop culture clues.

"Thanks, Sabby-apple," he says, penciling in the answer. While he's distracted, I check my voicemail. Considering the mountain of messages I've left Calvin this past week, his is strikingly brief. He wants to talk to me, he says. Tonight. His tone is neutral, allowing me no insight to his mood. I've been dying to talk to Calvin all week, but after my little psycho scene this morning, I don't trust myself to call him back. I'm liable to say something crazy.

So I text him instead. After a rapid firing of messages, I agree to meet Calvin for dinner at Ganesha's, an Indian restaurant downtown. I can't tell if I should be pleased with this arrangement. On the one hand, Calvin wouldn't ask me to dinner if he thinks I'm a complete psycho. On the other hand, we're meeting at a public place. You know, the kind of place you'd go if you were concerned you might be meeting a complete psycho.

"In my day," Dad says, "people actually used phones to call each other."

"Texting is quicker than calling," I say, slipping my phone back into my pocket. I'm dressed in my Adventure Pal uniform of khaki shorts and black polo, because, as far as Dad knows, I worked at the zoo today. I turn my attention back to the crossword puzzle, but Dad keeps looking at me. I start to feel self-conscious under his gaze.

"That was Michelle," I say, feeling the need to explain myself. "She wants to go to dinner tonight."

"When are we going to meet this Michelle?" Dad says. "The two of you seem to be pretty good friends."

I answer with a noncommittal shrug. Dad is never going to meet Michelle, because if he did, he would know that I've been lying to him. I'm definitely not Miss Popularity, but I don't think even Dad would believe that I've become BFFs with a soccer mom in her late thirties. But I don't have time to deal with this now, because in less than an hour I'm supposed to meet Calvin for dinner. And although I'm clueless as to why he wants to see me, I'm certain I'm not showing up in my present attire.

"I'm going to go change my clothes," I say, stealing out

of the kitchen before Dad can ask me any more questions. I rush into my bedroom and fling the closet door open, assessing my wardrobe. There, hanging before me like lifeless slabs of meat, are the usual suspects: T-shirts, solid polos, a few button-down blouses. There's a black-and-white striped cardigan and a tweed skirt Mom bought at Macy's that still has the tags on it. I rummage through my closet's pathetic offerings and start to panic. Nothing in this closet is going to turn Calvin's head.

And I want to. Turn his head, that is. No matter what happens tonight, I want to look good.

Fortunately for me, there is someone in this house who is kind of an expert in seduction. I take a deep breath and then creep down the hall toward Heather's bedroom.

"Heather," I say, tentatively knocking on her open door. She is sitting at the little white desk she's had since grade school, sketching. When she sees me she drops the pencil in her hand and flips over her sketchbook to hide whatever in the world it is she's working on. Who knows, maybe she's decided to take up drawing as a type of therapy.

"Hey Sabrina," she says, tucking a lock of hair behind her ear. "What's up?"

"Not much." I make my way past a mountain of dirty clothes and the Pack 'n Play where Brodie sleeps and sit primly on the edge of Heather's unmade bed. "What you working on?"

"Oh, nothing." She looks down at the desk and starts fidgeting with a tin of colored pencils, suddenly shy. "It's stupid, really."

"What is it?" I say, curious.

"Remember how, back in high school, I was kind of into art?"

I look at her blankly. Heather was into art? I have absolutely no memory of that.

"It was just my sophomore year, really," she says, "when I had art with Mr. Curtis. Anyway, I was actually pretty good at it—I was even considering taking AP, if you can believe it."

I can't.

"But then . . ." She doesn't have to continue her story. I'm guessing it ends the same way all of her stories end: with Thayne. I can't say I'm surprised. It's impossible for me to imagine Thayne hooking up with a chick enrolled in AP *anything*. He's the kind of guy who sees a girl with an IQ as a social liability.

Heather drops her head to her chest and I wonder if she isn't going to start crying. I'm not sure how to handle this open, vulnerable sister of mine. So I just sit there, on the edge of the bed, and cross my legs at the ankles, waiting for her to collect herself. Finally, she lifts her head and flips over the sketchbook.

"This," she says, handing the drawing to me, "is a mock-up. For the cover of Ginger & Ivory's fall catalogue. Geri, my boss, mentioned she wanted to go in a new direction with their 'artistic design,' and, I don't know, it sparked something inside of me."

The sketch is of two women, impossibly slim and chic and laden with lots and lots of pretty packages, strolling down a city sidewalk. The picture pops with color. There is something whimsical about the drawing—it is a unique combination of sophistication and playfulness.

"I love it," I say.

"I don't know," Heather says. "I probably won't show it to Geri."

"You have to. Honestly, Heather, this is really great."

"Thanks." Heather smiles at me. I didn't intend on currying her favor before asking her for help, but I'm guessing it can't hurt. I nervously uncross and then cross my legs again. Heather and I aren't the kind of sisters who typically swap wardrobes.

"Heather, I need your help. You know that guy I told you about?"

"The Fourth of July guy?"

"Yeah. Him. He just asked me to dinner, and I'd like to not show up dressed as an Adventure Pal."

To my utter amazement, Heather walks to her closet and seizes a low-cut, slinky black tank top and a pair of sleek embellished jeans. Then she gets on her hands and knees and starts rummaging through what must be a hundred pairs of shoes. She throws me a pair of strappy sandals with an intimidating three-inch heel. I'd protest this choice in footwear if it weren't for the fact that, at this point, I'm willing to try just about anything.

I throw on the clothes and then Heather whisks me into the bathroom. I sit patiently on the toilet seat while she attacks me with an arsenal of cosmetics. Heather is in her element. I'm reminded of those makeover shows I sometimes watch with Heather at night, where some bespectacled, frumpy disaster of a woman is transformed into a hot fashionista. Maybe that's why I start to hold pretty high expectations for my own transformation. I'm a Chapstick and mascara kind of girl, but maybe with Heather's help, I really will look, you know, fabulous. Maybe, with Heather's help, I really will be able to blow Calvin away tonight.

"Okay, Sabrina," Heather says when she finishes my makeup. "What do you think?"

This is the moment of truth. If I were the frumpy disaster of a woman on one of those makeover shows, this is the part where the cosmetician would swivel me around in my chair to face the mirror, and I, viewing the new and improved version of myself, would inevitably burst into tears. Now, in real life, in this completely untelevised makeover, when I see myself in the mirror I do, in fact, want to cry. But not for the reason you'd think.

"So," Heather says, "how'd I do?"

I take another look in the mirror, trying to find myself beneath layers of foundation, blush, and eyeliner.

"I look like a hussy," I say.

Heather gives my shoulders a quick squeeze and smiles. "Exactly."

. . . .

The problem with wearing three-inch heels is they make walking next to impossible. I find this out after I parallel park my Corolla in front of Ganesha's and hobble across the sidewalk toward Calvin. I'm hoping that I don't look as ridiculous as I feel.

"Hey," Calvin says, graciously offering me his arm. He is casually dressed in a T-shirt, jeans, and Converse sneakers.

"What's the occasion?"

I refrain from removing one of my awful shoes and stabbing him. Instead, I just shrug my shoulders like the fool that I am, and, leaning heavily on Calvin's arm, totter into the restaurant. The hostess greets us with a bright smile and promptly ushers us to a table.

"So," Calvin says, taking a seat, "how've you been?"

There are a hundred different ways to answer to this question. Miserable. Heartsick. Insane. Desperate.

"Okay," I lie. "I'm glad to see you finally figured out how to use your phone."

"Yeah," he says, giving me a sheepish smile. "I meant to call you earlier, it's just . . . I've been busy."

"Busy? Busy doing what?"

"Filling in at the Game Shack, for starters. But, of course, you already know that."

I'm certain that even the mountain of makeup I'm wearing can't disguise the fact that my face is burning. Before I have a chance to explain myself, Calvin continues.

"I've also started working for my aunt. Turns out, I'm going to need to earn more than just fifty bucks to pay for fall semester."

"Oh," I say, digesting this bit of information. Maybe things aren't as bleak as I've imagined. Maybe Calvin hasn't been avoiding me. Maybe he really has been busy.

"What kind of work are you doing?"

"Nothing glamorous. My aunt owns a small business, and I'm her new designated gopher. Her store is actually just around the corner. That's how I discovered Ganesha's."

"My sister works down here too," I say. "She just got a job cashiering at a little boutique called Ginger & Ivory."

"Hum," Calvin says. "How's your sister doing, anyway? I bet she's pretty upset that her ex-boyfriend is getting married."

"How did you know about that?"

"It's all over Facebook," Calvin says.

I guess I shouldn't be surprised by his answer. After all, Thayne Stockett and Jordan Greene are local celebrities. Still, I feel unreasonably bothered that Calvin knows so much about Heather's love life.

Thankfully, our waitress arrives, rattling off the dinner specials and preventing any further discussion of Heather. Our waitress is in her late twenties, Indian, and very pretty. She's wearing a canary yellow sari that, loose-fitting as it is, still can't hide the fact that she has a great figure. After she fills our glasses with ice water she crosses her arms beneath her very ample chest and makes small talk with Calvin. I feign interest in the utterly indecipherable menu in front of me, pretending not to notice that Calvin is openly flirting with her. When she finally walks back to the kitchen, he actually turns around to watch her.

"Sorry," he says, repositioning himself in his chair. "I kind of have a thing for older women."

Once again, I refrain from removing one of my shoes and stabbing him. We endure an agonizing moment of silence. There is so much I want to say to Calvin, but now that I have the chance, I can't bring myself to say anything at all.

"Do you know what you want?" he finally says.

After so much silence has preceded it, his question

catches me off guard. It takes me a moment to connect his question to the menu in front of me.

The menu. He is talking about the menu.

"I don't know," I say, meeting his gaze. I look into his beautiful eyes and try not to whimper. "I've never had Indian food."

"You've never had Indian food? Where are you from?"

"Here."

"Hey," he says, picking up on my defeated tone, "it's not the worst place to be from."

"Maybe not," I say, "but it kind of feels like the worst place to stay."

"I take it you've decided not to go to Caltech then?"

Is that what I've decided? It's funny, because I don't recall deciding anything at all. This is just one of those decisions that somehow has been made for me.

"I guess so. Things didn't exactly work out as I'd planned."

"The best laid plans of mice and men . . ."

"Thank you, Mr. Steinbeck."

This, I remind myself, is why I like Calvin. He's the kind of guy who can drop literary references into everyday conversation.

"So if I ever decide to stop by your house again, your dad's not going to shoot me down?"

"No," I say. "But that's only because he doesn't own a shotgun." Mom may very well make me file a restraining order against Calvin, but I decline to volunteer this information. I don't want to deflate the hope that is ballooning inside of me. My lips spread into a wide smile. Is Calvin saying what I think he's saying? Does he really want to keep seeing me? And if he does, how would that work exactly? What would I tell my parents if Calvin showed up at my house again?

I don't have the faintest idea how I'd explain Calvin to my parents. But that doesn't matter. Right now, all I want to do is persuade Calvin that a future that includes the two of us is possible.

"Calvin, the whole stalker thing didn't work out. If my parents thought you were a stalker, I wouldn't, you know, be planning on staying in Boise."

"That is good to hear." The balloon of hope within me expands so much I can hardly breathe. "Since you're staying, you really should consider joining Game Club. We meet on Wednesday nights at the Game Shack. If you're not doing anything this Wednesday, you should swing by."

"Maybe I will," I say, encouraged by his offer. I smile at him and then look at the menu. "So, what's good here?"

"I like all of the curries. Especially the chicken coconut. The tandoori's really good too. So is the shrimp masala."

I don't know what any of these entrees are. At the moment, I don't really care. I'm just happy that things seem to be going okay. Better than okay. I straighten myself up on my chair and beam across the table at Calvin.

But, as the saying goes, all good things come to an end.

"So," Calvin says, "what's with the new face?"

"My sister did my makeup."

"Your sister did your makeup? Why?"

There is, of course, no point in answering this question. Calvin already knows the answer. He can see right through me. I am trying too hard. This is nothing new. I've been trying too hard my whole life.

I am suddenly very, very tired.

I lay the menu down on the table and rub my eyes, even though, given the amount of eyeliner I'm wearing, I'm bound to end up looking like a raccoon.

"So, I see on Facebook that you're in a relationship," Calvin says. "Who's the lucky guy?"

And the hits keep coming. I look at him in disbelief. Is he really going to make me answer this question?

"I just thought, after last weekend . . ."

"Last weekend was fun. But we're not in a relationship, Sabrina. I need us to be clear about that. It's nothing personal. I'm just not, you know, real big on commitment."

I cannot respond to this. Presently, I am using all of my energy to keep myself from crying.

"I don't want to hurt you, Sabrina."

I huff out a bitter laugh. It's a little late for that.

"This is about Alex, isn't it?" I say.

"Alex? This has nothing to do with Alex." He leans back in his chair and folds his arms across his chest. "If this is about anyone, it's about me."

I can't believe I'm getting the "it's not you, it's me" act from Calvin. The worst part is that I can tell that he's really trying to sell me this line. Well, sorry, Calvin. I'm not buying it.

Our waitress returns, her cheery demeanor in stark contrast with my dark mood. She tucks a loose strand of glossy black hair behind her ear and whips out a small spiral notebook.

141

"You two ready to order?" she asks.

"You bet," Calvin says.

"Is this going to be together or separate?"

Calvin gives me a quick, darting glance across the table. Then he turns his full attention to the beautiful woman at his side.

"Separate," Calvin says, without the faintest hint of hesitation.

Chapter 21

Heather is watching TV when I come home from Ganesha's. I join her in the family room and slump down on the couch, even though The Noise is crying at full capacity. At the moment, I can't bear the thought of being alone.

Heather is standing just inches from the TV screen, presumably in an effort to actually hear something besides Brodie's cries. She has the baby on her hip and is bouncing up and down, and, to my surprise, actually laughing.

"What are you watching?" I say.

"It's a new sketch show," she says, bobbing toward me. "This guy I work with told me about it. It's pretty funny."

Heather sits next to me on the couch and sets Brodie on her knees. She wags the remote in front of him and he thankfully takes the bait and shoves it in his mouth. Now that he's quieted down a bit, I turn my attention to the TV. A new skit has just started, and one of the actors looks very familiar.

"Is that who I think it is?" I say.

"Yeah," Heather says. "That's Jeff Goldblum. It must be a cameo or something—he's not normally on the show."

Usually, I'd go all cuckoo for Cocoa Puffs over Jeff Goldblum, but tonight I just can't summon the energy. Maybe it's because this current version of Jeff Goldblum is still tall, but, you know, not quite so dark and handsome. His hair, in fact, is gray. Not graying. Gray. I study him for a moment, and find it hard to believe that this is the man of my dreams.

"He's hilarious," Heather says.

"He's old." I rip the remote from Brodie's chubby hands and change the channel. Brodie, of course, starts bawling again. I guess I can't really be too upset with him, because I'm bawling too.

"Sabrina." Heather clutches Brodie to her chest and scoots toward me. She puts her arm around me and I easily give in to her attempt to console me and rest my head on her shoulder.

"Tonight was a disaster," I say between sobs.

"Do you want to talk about it?"

I do. As humiliating as my dinner with Calvin was, I do want to talk about it. And the incredible thing is, someone actually wants to listen to me talk. Once I start talking to Heather, I can't stop. I tell her about Ganesha's, and then about stalking Calvin at the Game Shack, and then about how I scaled the water tower with Calvin on the Fourth of July. I talk until Brodie has passed out in Heather's arms. I talk until the gray light peeping in through the blinds gives way to blackness. The words just keep coming, tirelessly, effortlessly. I never knew I had so many words inside of me before.

I tell Heather about how Calvin held me at Starbucks, and about the first time he surprised me at the zoo, and then, when I finally stop to catch my breath, she asks me about the one thing I'm not sure I want to discuss.

"How did you meet this guy anyway?" Heather says.

There's a reason I've been telling this story backwards.

"We went to Skyview together." Heather narrows her eyes at me. She knows my history vis-a-vis the opposite sex.

"Okay. But, like, how did you two hook up? I mean, I *know* you two weren't hanging out in high school. What made Mr. Fourth of July suddenly appear?"

There's no easy way to say this. I decide the most painless way is just to do it fast—like ripping off a Band-Aid.

"I paid him to stalk me," I say.

"Mr. Fourth of July is your stalker?" Heather says. She's silent for a moment, taking it all in. "Why?"

"Because I wanted to go to Caltech, and I figured if Dad thought I had a stalker here, maybe he wouldn't think it was such a bad idea for me to move away."

"But you're not going to Caltech," Heather says.

"Caltech doesn't know that. In the spring, I notified the school that I was planning on attending."

"Why didn't you just tell Mom and Dad that? Why did you lie to them?"

After a warm and fuzzy evening of sharing, Heather's question strikes me as especially harsh. I fold my arms across my chest, suddenly regretting my decision to go all confessional.

"For the same reason you lied to Paul," I say. "We both wanted something that we didn't deserve."

Heather's face hardens. I'm afraid that she might actually slap me. Given the circumstances, I think she'd be justified.

But she doesn't hit me. She just stares vacantly at the floor, and then turns to me with glassy eyes.

"Why don't you deserve to go to Caltech?"

This is one facet of my life that I'm not too eager to delve into. I avoid Heather's gaze and shrug my shoulders.

"Tell me," she says. "Why don't you deserve to go to Caltech?"

"Because Mom and Dad don't think I'm worth the expense."

"For being so smart, that's a pretty dumb thing to say."

"It's true. When it comes to you and Tyler, no expense is too great. Tyler muddled through high school, but still Mom went to work so they could afford to send him to that fancy private college in Washington. And you, you move back home on a moment's notice, and Mom and Dad rearrange their whole lives to accommodate you, just like that. But I can't inconvenience them. I'm not allowed that luxury."

"What on earth are you talking about?" Heather says.

"Don't pretend like you don't know," I say.

"I don't know. Maybe Mom and Dad don't want you to go to Caltech, but it's not because they don't think you're worth it. If anything, it's because they don't want to be separated from the only good child they have."

"I'm not their only good child."

"Oh, come on. We both know Tyler's a complete loser," Heather says, smiling. "And I'm almost thirty and still living at home. With two illegitimate children. And, like, absolutely no prospects. I guess what I'm saying is, if any of us deserves anything, it's you."

"Well, I wish Mom and Dad thought so too."

"Seems to me, this isn't about what Mom and Dad think."

"Then what is it about?"

"You."

She, of course, is entirely wrong. But I don't bother arguing with her, because I can tell she thinks she's just said something incredibly insightful.

"But you were right about one thing," Heather says. "I don't deserve Paul."

"Heather . . ." I start, but she cuts me off with a wave of her hand.

"In the two weeks I was with Paul, he gave me more compliments than Thayne ever did. He didn't just make me feel like I could be a better person. When I was with him, I was better, you know? It was like all the crap I went through with Thayne never happened."

I look at my beautiful sister and the dark-haired baby sleeping in her arms and my heart starts to hurt. She's not just mourning the loss of Paul, she's mourning something even more heartbreaking—lost possibility.

"We kind of got off track, didn't we?" she says. "We weren't talking about my pathetic love life. We were talking about yours."

Suddenly, my Calvin drama seems incredibly trivial.

"You know what I'd do if I were you?" Heather says.

"What?"

"Rebound."

I cast another glance at Brodie and try not to smirk. I know I shouldn't be taking dating advice from Heather, but still, I have a fleeting thought of Joe. I'm still kicking myself for not accepting his lunch offer earlier today. This, of course, is nonsense. Even if I wanted to, you know, go on the rebound, Joe wouldn't be the kind of guy I'd call. He's much more than a consolation prize.

"I'm not going to go on the rebound."

"Well, I am," Heather says. "This guy I work with asked me out."

"Heather." I don't even attempt to disguise my alarm. When Heather goes on the rebound, there tend to be consequences.

"It's nothing serious. He's younger than me. And he's not at all my type. He's into philosophy and all that junk. In fact," she says, giving me a sly smile, "you'd probably like him."

"So are you going to go out with him?"

"Probably," Heather says. "I need to do something to take my mind off . . . everything. And this guy at work . . . he's not really into taking things too seriously."

"He sounds like a real winner."

"He's not. But he is kind of like the perfect recovery guy. Tell you what. After I use him, I'll pass him onto you."

I give Heather a courtesy smile, but frankly, I don't see this happening. Maybe Heather and I aren't as different as I used to think, but I can't fathom a reality where we'd actually go out with the same guy.

Chapter 22

The housing deposit for Caltech is due on Friday. Like, three days from today Friday. This, essentially, is the content of the third and final email I receive from the college's housing department Tuesday night. I stare at the computer screen, reading the email over and over again, and let the severity of my situation settle over me.

If, by this Friday, I haven't paid the $2,500 housing deposit, I'm not going to Caltech.

I'd like to discuss this predicament with Heather, but Heather, unfortunately, is at work and not due home for another half an hour. Her absence is doubly missed as I am stuck watching Brodie while Mom prepares dinner. I shift the baby in my lap and check out Facebook to kill time. Calvin has posted a message on my wall that says *Boise State Game Club Needs You!* I had almost forgotten about his invitation to the Game Shack tomorrow night. I can't tell if this reminder leaves me feeling elated or a little bit annoyed.

I'm going to have to go ahead and say annoyed.

My attendance at Caltech may still be up in the air, but I can say with complete confidence that I will not be at the Game Shack tomorrow night. I've had about all I can take of Calvin Kleinstein.

Brodie is getting restless, so I abandon the computer and its horrible notifications and wander into the kitchen. Mom is at the island, dicing a red pepper for a Caesar salad.

"Sabrina," she says, wagging the knife in her hand at me, "set the table."

The menacing way she's thrusting the knife in my direction prevents me from arguing with her. I balance Brodie on my hip and head for the cupboard.

"Bowls or plates?" I ask.

"Bowls." Mom dumps the discarded pieces of the red pepper into the sink. She turns on the faucet and flips on the disposal, which, surprise surprise, sets Brodie off. I proceed to simultaneously soothe him and set the table. I'm not doing a very good job at either—a fact that doesn't escape Mom's notice.

"The napkin goes on the left, Sabrina." Left, right, who cares? Mom does, of course. I begrudgingly move the napkin I've just set down to the left side of the bowl. When it comes to place settings, Mom demands perfection.

Mom sets the diced red pepper aside and moves on to deboning a rotisserie chicken. I open the utensil drawer and count out five forks, watching Mom as she meticulously dissects the withered rotisserie chicken on the counter. Mom's ability to extract every last piece of meat from the bone is very nearly a party trick. I know from experience that she will attack that bird until there's nothing left but a useless carcass.

"Forks on the left too?" I say. I've set the table enough times to know this, but I am suddenly unsure of myself.

Mom gives me a confirming nod without looking up

from her work. I walk around the table, placing each fork on the center of each napkin. I can't stop thinking about the email I just received. Unless I act fast, my dream of going to Caltech will be just that. A dream.

Maybe Heather was right. Maybe honesty is the best policy. Maybe, if I just turn to Mom and confess right now, everything will work out.

Still juggling Brodie in my arms, I face Mom. She has already finished ripping apart the chicken and is removing the packaging from a head of iceberg lettuce. She discards the cellophane and then, without warning, smacks the lettuce against the countertop. In one deft movement she plucks out the stem and tosses it aside. I look from Mom to the truncated stalk, all bone white and tissuey, like a broken spinal cord.

There is no way I'm telling this woman I lied to her.

"I talked to Gayle Davis's husband today," she says. "He's a district court judge."

I don't like where this is headed.

"I told him about your . . . situation," Mom says, "and he said it would be a good idea to file a restraining order. Well, he said technically, it's not a restraining order, but a stalking injunction. Anyway," Mom says, wiping her hands on a dish towel, "Gayle's husband said that as long as you've been stalked at least two times and the stalking has caused you or your family distress, the court will grant an injunction. Tomorrow I need you to go to the administration office at the zoo and get the name and address of this man who's been stalking you. Then, on Wednesday, we can both go to the courthouse and get this taken care of. Unless," she says, eyeballing me, "there's some reason you've been putting this off."

Um, yeah, there's a reason I've been putting this off. A big reason. But Mom doesn't know this. Or does she?

"I just don't know if filing a stalking injunction or whatever is such a good idea," I say. "I mean, this guy knows where I live. What if he gets served papers and goes completely berserk? He could come here and, you know, kill me or something."

This is the kind of argument that would work on Dad. Mom, however, is not moved by my appeal to emotion. She doesn't want to file a restraining order because she's concerned about my safety. She wants to file a restraining order as a matter of principle.

"He's not going to come here and kill you," she says. I suppose I should be reassured by this, but really, I'm insulted. It's like Mom thinks my life is so inconsequential that no one would actually take the trouble to come and murder me.

Mom turns her attention back to making dinner. I rack my brain for a way out of this predicament, but come up with nothing. I know one thing for certain—I cannot file a court-ordered stalking injunction against Calvin. It's one thing to lie to my parents; it's another thing entirely to lie to the state of Idaho.

Mom has started ripping the iceberg lettuce into bite-sized squares when the phone rings.

"Sabrina." Mom glances toward the phone. I pick up the receiver and look at the caller ID.

"It's Thayne," I say.

"Don't answer," Mom says. "I already talked to him today. He's looking for Heather—he wants to set up a time for Jordan to meet Mack. Thayne said Heather won't return any of the messages he's left on her cell."

"I don't blame her," I say.

"Whether she likes it or not, Heather can't just hide from this." Mom grimaces. "I don't know why both of you girls ended up being so passive-aggressive."

I have an idea, but I keep my mouth shut.

"There's Heather now," Mom says at the sound of the garage door opening. Heather bursts in the door, clutching a portfolio, her oversized purse slung in the crook of her arm.

"Your ex-boyfriend's been calling," Mom calls out.

Poor Heather. I can tell Mom's in the mood to lay into her about Thayne. If I could, I'd do something to spare her. But, as luck would have it, Heather ends up saving herself.

"Guess what?" she says, ignoring Mom altogether and waving the portfolio in her hand. She breezes into the kitchen, swiping Brodie from my arms and planting a big kiss on his forehead. She turns her back to Mom and lays the portfolio on the table.

"Geri loved my mock-up! She's going to use it as the cover art for the fall catalogue."

Heather opens the portfolio and pulls out a finished copy of the illustration I saw a few nights ago.

"Heather!" I say, giving her a tight sideways hug. "That's great!"

"What's this?" Mom wanders over to the table and peers over Heather's shoulder. She studies the illustration for a moment and then listens as Heather gives a detailed explanation of its genesis. Clearly, the good news has an effect on Mom. The case of Thayne Stockett and the missed phone calls is dropped entirely. When Dad comes home just moments later, Mom plasters the illustration to his chest while recounting Heather's story practically word for word.

Mom and Dad are so high on the news of Heather's success that when she tells them she's planning on going out with a guy from work tomorrow night, they quickly agree to watch the kids. She, of course, doesn't mention that the guy she's going out with is, in her words, a perfect recovery guy. I raise my eyebrows at her and she grins back at me.

Dad, noticing this exchange, pats me on the back. He is clearly pleased that his daughters are finally being friendly with each other.

We settle down at the dinner table and enjoy an unusually pleasant meal together. The only hiccup of the night occurs when Mom decides to revisit the whole stalker issue.

"Don," Mom says, "I spoke to Rob Davis today about Sabrina's stalker. He said we should definitely file a restraining order. I told Sabrina that we're going to the courthouse on Wednesday to get it taken care of."

Heather shoots me a concerned look across the table.

"And I told Mom," I say, turning to Dad, "that I don't think that's such a good idea. I mean, I haven't even seen that guy in weeks. I really don't think it's even a problem anymore."

"Sabrina," Mom says. "Rob Davis is a district court judge. I think he knows better than you whether filing an injunction is a good idea."

"It just makes me really uncomfortable," I say, about to cry. "I mean, I don't think this guy is even a threat any more."

"Rob Davis thinks he's a threat," Mom says.

"Cindy," Dad says, obviously sensing my increasing distress.

"Like it or not, we need to file that injunction," Mom says.

Poor me. I can tell Mom's not about to let this go. If I could, I'd do something to save myself. But, remarkably, wonderfully, Heather comes to my rescue.

"Oh, Mom, lay off," Heather says. "If Sabrina doesn't think he's a threat, then he's not a threat."

"Fine." Mom sighs. "But if I see that man one more time, I'm going to go to the zoo and get his name and address myself."

If I could, I'd hoist Heather on my shoulders and give three cheers. Instead, I mouth "thank you" to her across the table. As far as I'm concerned, this problem has been solved. After all, Calvin's already served me the "it's not you, it's me" line. I really don't think he's going to be driving past our house anytime soon.

After dinner, Dad suggests we go for ice cream. We all scramble into the Tahoe and head for McDonald's. We order vanilla cones and Cokes and sit at the little round tables outside. It is one of those impossibly golden summer evenings. It's the kind of evening that makes it easy to believe that nothing could possibly go wrong. I lick my ice cream cone and laugh and let the subdued warmth encompass me, completely unprepared for the mayhem that is about to come my way.

Chapter 23

I spend the next day in Adventure Pal purgatory. This, really, should be the first glaring sign that things are about to go horribly awry. For my entire shift, I am stationed at the Nature's Nightmares exhibit. The exhibit is located in an ancient greenhouse near the south entrance that used to house a butterfly garden, until all the butterflies died. Since then, the greenhouse has been used for temporary exhibits only—last year it had a Komodo dragon on loan from the Indianapolis Zoo, and the year before that it boasted a shallow pool full of stingrays. Due to budgetary constraints, this year's exhibit is on the cheap. Aside from some fruit bats and a turkey vulture, Nature's Nightmares is primarily a bug showcase: dung beetles, cockroaches, scorpions, a goliath bird-eating spider, and a black widow.

Aside from training, this is the first time that I've been assigned to this post. It's common knowledge among the Adventure Pals that this is the absolute worst place to be stationed, and I quickly figure out why. It's not just the stifling heat that gets to you. It's the isolation. The exhibit just isn't that big of a draw. People come to the zoo for, you know, the lions and tigers and bears. Not the insects.

So, basically, I spend my shift alone, surrounded by creeping, crawling creatures. Maybe this is why my own thoughts transform into creeping, crawling things themselves, buzzing around my brain like a full-on infestation. I think about the impending deadline for the housing deposit at Caltech. I think about the lies I've told my parents. I think about the lunch I almost had with Joe from Omaha. I think about Calvin and the way he made a fool of me at Ganesha's.

And then, I think about the way he kissed me on the Fourth of July, and every neuron and wire inside of my brain feels like it is being gnawed to bits.

Late afternoon, I have visitors. A woman with a handful of children enters the greenhouse and marches toward me. Her thick blonde hair is held back from her face with a fabric headband. She is wearing a crisp white blouse and pleated shorts. She speaks to me in clipped, enunciated words.

She wants me to give her and her brood a tour of the exhibit. I want to tear the fabric headband off her head and muzzle her.

But, of course, I behave myself and stick to my talking points. I point out the dung beetles and talk about how they feed exclusively on feces. I describe how the turkey vulture's keen sense of smell allows him to detect the gasses of decay in dead animals. By the time we reach the black widow, the woman in the headband isn't looking so good. When I state that the name "black widow" comes from the fact that the female eats the male after mating, the woman in the headband has heard enough.

"These are children!" she says, cupping her hands over her youngest child's ears.

Needless to say, our impromptu tour is, thankfully, terminated.

The woman and her children file out of the stuffy greenhouse, and I am once again left alone with my thoughts. I am still standing in front of the black widow, simmering up a nice pot of thought stew, when my cell phone buzzes.

I read the text message from Calvin: *Game Shack. Tonight. 6:30.*

I read the message again. For some reason, I had thought the meeting was at seven. Six thirty, seven, what's the difference? I'm not going anyway.

I slip my phone back into my pocket. And then, moments later, it buzzes again.

It's another message from Calvin: *NEED U 2 come.*

Despite the heat and the isolation and the creeping, crawling bugs, I somehow am blessed with a mental breakthrough. I look at the message on my phone and I can suddenly identify the reason that my life has gone off the rails. There's a reason that I've told so many lies to my parents. There's a reason that my plot to go to Caltech has so miserably failed. There's a reason that I'm stuck here, in a hot, stuffy bubble, with absolutely no chance of escaping.

And that reason is Calvin.

I peer through the glass at the black widow dancing on her web. The red hourglass on her bulbous abdomen strikes me as significant. Usually, I regard this venomous spider and her violent mating ritual with disgust. But not today. Today, the black widow and I are simpatico.

It is as if the soupy heat has suddenly evaporated from the building. With uncharacteristic composure, I respond to Calvin's text. Then I pocket my phone and smile a mirthless smile. One of us is going to be destroyed by this relationship. And it's not going to be me.

. . . .

I head for the Game Shack directly after work. I'm dressed in my sweaty Adventure Pal uniform, complete with safari hat, but I don't bother to stop home first and get gussied up. I'm bent on destruction, not seduction. Frankly, I don't really care what Calvin thinks of me, as long as he knows exactly what I think of him.

As I drive, I fantasize about the scene that is about to go down. The whole daydream is melodramatic and improbable and immensely satisfying. I'll storm into the Game Shack, where the entire Game Club presidency will be assembled like a quorum of elders, dressed in blue blazers and wearing tortoiseshell frames. In an affected English accent, I'll rip into Calvin, listing all the horrors he has inflicted on me with unflinching detail. Calvin will attempt, and fail, to defend himself. Gavels will pound. Calvin's peers will denounce him as a cad and demand his immediate resignation as Game Club president.

I think I let myself become so absorbed in this absurd mental movie because I have absolutely no idea what I'm doing. All I know is that I'm angry. In fact, by the time I pull my Corolla into the Game Shack's parking lot, I am very nearly blind with rage. My vision is not the only thing that's malfunctioning. My body is funneling so much energy into fueling my anger that other things start shutting down too. Like my ability to walk straight. And my capacity to, you know, reason.

When I enter the store, I take in my surroundings with my nearly useless eyes. I can't see Calvin anywhere. In fact, I can't see anyone at all, except a dorky-looking guy standing behind the counter. I walk toward him and grasp the edge of the counter in an attempt to prevent myself from collapsing.

"Where's Calvin?" I say.

"Calvin?" the guy says, taking a noticeable step away from me. "Who's Calvin?"

I take a deep breath and try to focus.

"Brad," I say. "Brad Klein. You know, the Game Club president."

"Oh," the guy says. "Him." He tilts his head to one side and glances over his shoulder. "Hey Alex," he yells, "we've got another customer here who wants to talk to your boyfriend."

"He's not my boyfriend," a young woman calls back. I peek over the dorky guy's shoulder to see Alex walking toward me. She's wearing sandals and an ankle-length floral skirt and a white tank top that shows off her tattoo. It's the kind of outfit that no one in this day and age should be able to pull off, but somehow, on her, it looks amazing. Alex walks around the counter and stands right in front of me, crossing her tanned arms across her petite frame. Her skin is, simply, luminous. Her Facebook photos don't do her justice.

"Let me guess," she says, giving me a good once-over. "Brad sold you the game board with the missing pieces."

"What?"

"You're not the customer who called earlier? About *Carcassonne?*"

"No," I say. "I'm here for Game Club."

"Oh," she says, grabbing my hand and laughing. "You just look so . . . crazed. Brad covered for me last night and he apparently tampered with the merchandise. He took, like, half of the pieces out of a game he sold to some woman."

"Why?"

"Because," she says, her eyes dancing, "he likes to screw with people. But, I guess if you know Brad, you know that already."

The only thing I know right now is that I'm not going to find an ally in Alex. It's obvious that Calvin's habit of acting like a jerk delights her. I shrug my shoulders and look down at my hiking boots, and then stare at Alex's dainty sandaled feet. Her toenails are painted a bright aqua blue. For some reason, the sight of those perfectly polished toes nearly brings me to tears.

What on earth am I doing here?

"So you're here for the meeting?" Alex asks.

"Yeah."

"You know it doesn't start until seven, right?"

I look at my watch. It is just now half past six. Calvin may like to screw with people, but what would be his motivation for telling me to come early?

"Are you sure?" I say.

"I'm sure," Alex says, gesturing at the empty store to prove her point.

"Brad," I force myself to say, "told me six thirty. We're friends from high school. Maybe he told me to come early so we could, you know, catch up before the meeting."

It's an unlikely theory, one that Alex clearly isn't buying. But it's the dorky guy behind the counter who discredits me altogether.

"Brad's not even coming tonight," he says. "He's going out with some woman."

"Tell me it's not the skank he hooked up with on the Fourth?" Alex says, turning to him.

"No. I'm pretty sure he ended that."

"Good," Alex says. "That chick was crazy."

Um, objection?

"He said he's going out with someone he met at work," the guy says. Obviously, keeping tabs on Calvin's social calendar is the highlight of this guy's life. "She's like, thirty or something and has a couple kids."

"He's going out with the cougar?" Alex says, her eyes widening.

"What?" the guy says. "It's not that gross. I looked her up on Facebook. She's hot."

"The cougar's the skank's sister," Alex says.

"The cougar's the skank's sister?" the guy says.

The cougar's the skank's sister. I reach for the counter again. If my vision was bad before, it is completely impaired now. For a brief moment, everything goes black. Alex rushes to my side and places her hand on the small of my back. She is assaulting me with questions about my condition, but I can't answer her. I squeeze my eyes together, waiting for the dizzy spell to pass.

When I finally open my eyes, everything is suddenly clear.

"I'm the skank," I say. I don't wait around to see how Alex and the dorky guy react to this bombshell. Heather is about to go out with Calvin. And that absolutely cannot happen. I have to go home, and now.

. . . .

Heather and Mom are sitting on the front porch, waiting, when I pull into the driveway. I experience a brief moment of relief. There is still time. I slam the car door shut and cross the driveway toward the porch. That's when I notice that Heather is wearing the same slinky black top and sleek jeans I borrowed from her when I went to Ganesha's with Calvin. Only, on Heather, the outfit doesn't look ridiculous. It looks seductive. The fact that she is about to see Calvin dressed in what is essentially my breakup garb is too much for me. Suddenly, the focus of my anger transfers from Calvin to Heather. I mean, really. How could she?

I have just reached the base of the porch when it happens. Calvin shows up. My heart starts pounding. Sound is diminished. Time slows. The scene that follows changes everything, although it occurs in just a few seconds. I reach the base of the porch. *One thousand and one.* Calvin pulls up to the curb. *One thousand and two.* Mom leans into Heather and whispers something in her ear. *One thousand and three.* Heather looks at me. *One thousand and four.* I look at Calvin. *One thousand and five.*

Worlds collide.

Chapter 24

Calvin, of course, doesn't get out of the car. But he does find my gaze through the car window. Despite the fact that three women are staring him down, he doesn't look unnerved. In fact, just before he drives away, he curls his lips into a half smile and shrugs his shoulders, like he's a child who's just been caught with his hand in the cookie jar and expects to be loved for it anyway. It is this look that finally pushes me over the edge. It is this look that makes me decide to do the one thing I've been desperately trying to prevent from happening all along.

I flip around and face the porch, making a point not to look at Heather.

"I want to file a stalking injunction," I say.

"I should think so," Mom says.

I can feel the weight of Heather's eyes on me, but still I don't look at her. I'm not about to confess anything to Mom, and I'm pretty sure Heather's not going to either. It's one thing to go out with a skeezy guy in a rusted Ford Escort. It's another thing entirely to go out with your little sister's pretend stalker.

"Sabrina," Heather says, "think about what you're doing." It's funny, really, that she's the one reminding me to think before I act. I, of course, don't take her advice. I don't want to consider what will happen if I file a stalking injunction against Calvin. All I want to do is punish him. Now.

"She doesn't need to think about anything," Mom says, dismissing Heather with a wave of her hand. "That man has clearly crossed the line. Now, Sabrina, if you're okay, I'm going to go jot that plate number down, just in case we need it."

I give Mom a weak nod. As soon as she steps inside, Heather grabs my hand.

"Sabrina," she says, "I had no idea."

I flick my hand away from hers and fold my arms tightly against my chest. I'm in no mood for reconciliation.

"It's too bad you didn't get to recover tonight," I say.

"Sabrina—"

My heart is really pumping now. What I'm about to say may be the ugliest thing I've ever said, but I can't stop myself. This brand of anger doesn't come with brakes.

"I may have been unplanned, but you, Heather, you're the real mistake."

I hate that Calvin doesn't want me. I hate that Heather is prettier than me. But mostly, I hate that I can't take back the words I have just spat out. Heather makes an awful gulping sound, as if she is struggling to breathe, and then rushes past me into the house. The adrenaline that has been sustaining me evaporates, and I sink down to the front step and hold my head in my hands.

I don't know how long I sit on the front step, alone. All I know is that it is the middle of July and I am suddenly freezing. When Mom finally comes to find me I am shaking so violently that even my teeth are chattering. She takes me inside and drapes a blanket over my shoulders and sets me up on the couch in front of the TV. She makes me a bowl of Campbell's Chicken & Stars soup, just like she used to do when I was little, and sits beside me on the couch, making large circles on my back with the heel of her hand. When Dad comes home, he gets me a pair of socks from the laundry room and, when he has slipped the socks onto the ice cubes that are my feet, he takes Mom's place beside me on the couch.

Mom calls Rob Davis, the district court judge, and then calls the police department with Calvin's plate number. She types something up on the computer and then slips the printed documents into a manila folder. Usually, I start to panic when Mom takes charge, but tonight her assertiveness is something of a relief. Tomorrow I will file a stalking injunction against Calvin, but tonight Mom's the one doing all the work. For a moment, at least, I can still pretend that I am blameless.

Mom fluffs a pillow and slips it behind my head and gets me another bowl of soup. Then she joins Dad and me on the couch and we all watch a rerun of Seinfeld. I am the only one who's actually watching the show. Dad keeps glancing at me with concern, and Mom keeps asking me if I need anything. It hits me that I finally have exactly what I've always wanted—my parents' full and undivided attention.

I don't want to consider the price I've paid for this flash of attention. And so I don't. Instead I snuggle into the blanket, sigh in contentment, and then slip into a deep sleep. I'm going to need my rest. Unless I am mercifully struck down by some blessed act of God, tomorrow I'm going to the courthouse.

Chapter 25

A nd so, it comes to this: Mom and I huddled together in a waiting room, clipboards balanced on knees, completing the paperwork to file a stalking injunction against one Brad "Calvin" Klein. When I commenced Operation Stalker, I had kind of figured it would land me in California, not the courthouse. I never intended on taking the whole stalker thing this far.

So much for planning.

I look up from the paperwork and glance around me. Mom, in her sharp Ann Taylor pantsuit and Nine West heels, looks terribly out of place. As do I. The majority of the women here are well past adolescence. There are several Hispanic women, dark-haired and demure, most attached to a child or two. The rest of the room's occupants are a study in contrasts: blonde highlights and black roots, Daisy Dukes and cellulite, tight blouses and saggy chests, vibrant lipstick and yellowed teeth. I look around and remind myself that I am here because I have a pretend stalker. Emphasis on "pretend." The people in the waiting room are not pretending—they are real women with real problems. And real stalkers.

One of whom is seated next to me. I look over at the

guy, who is apparently under the delusion that jean cut-off shorts and sleeveless T-shirts are an appropriate clothing combo. I am not immune to the fact that he is unabashedly staring at me. When my eyes meet his he gives me a lewd smile and then laces his fingers together and places his hands behind his head, revealing twin tufts of mouse-brown armpit hair.

Yuck.

I know that Mr. Armpit Hair is indeed a real, legitimate stalker because I overheard him talking to the receptionist about the terms of his stalking injunction when he came in. I presume that the rest of the men in the waiting room, particularly the middle-aged gentleman in a Hawaiian shirt and aviator sunglasses, are also stalkers. It seems absurd to force the stalkers and the stalked into such close proximity. Mr. Armpit Hair leers at me again, and I consider asking Mom for an antiseptic wipe. Being here is like going to see the doctor for a well visit. If I'm not careful, I'm liable to pick something up.

Mom nudges me with her elbow and I return my attention to the clipboard in my lap. I am on page one of a five-page Request for Civil Stalking Injunction form. Under item one, "Petitioner (person needing protection)," I write my name and address. When I come to item two, "Respondent (person you need to be protected from)," I stall. As far as Mom knows, I don't know my stalker's name. But I pause for more than just this. I'm starting to wonder if the person I need to be protected from is myself.

I hastily flip through the rest of the form, looking for some kind of escape clause. I'm kind of wishing that I had heeded Heather's words of reason last night. I mean, I am about to complete a form that requires me to swear and notarize that Calvin stalked me. As mad as I am at Calvin, I don't know if his actions are worth committing perjury over.

I scour the form in my lap, searching for a miracle. I can't file a stalking injunction against Calvin. I also can't let Mom know that I've lied to her.

And then, I find it. On the bottom of page two, I read:

"Note! In addition to your own statements in this Request, you must provide some other evidence of stalking, like police reports, sworn statements from witnesses, audiotapes, photos, letters, etc."

I sigh with relief. Mercifully, in my case, there are no police reports, photos, or letters. There is no evidence of stalking, because I'm not being stalked.

Mom, who is hawking over my every move, notices the text I am reading and, as if on cue, whips out a manila file folder from her purse. She flips it open and produces the documents she printed out last night. There is a page with Calvin's personal information, including his address and driver's license number—information, Mom explains, she got from the police department last night. This, at least, I expected. The other two items in the folder are a bit more alarming. One is a document titled "Sworn Statement from Witness," signed by Mom, detailing the dates and times that she saw Calvin "stalk" me. The second is a grainy photo of Calvin parked in front of our house in his Ford Escort.

"Where did you get this?" I ask.

"I took it," Mom says, "on my phone. It's from the night Dad and I went to see *Seven Brides for Seven Brothers*, remember?"

"Yeah," I say. I have a clear recollection of that evening. I knew that the Calvin-sighting had made Dad panic, but I always figured it hadn't had much of an effect on Mom. "Why did you take a picture of him?"

"Instinct," Mom says. "Even in the dark, I could tell that man was up to no good."

"Oh," I say, processing this information.

"Why do you look so surprised?" Mom asks.

"I guess I never thought you worried about me."

"Of course I worry about you." She reaches for my hand and gives it a tight squeeze. I look at the photo of Calvin in my lap, and if it weren't so damning, I'd find it touching. It's not just evidence of stalking. It's proof of Mom's concern.

"Let me help you with that," Mom says, taking the clipboard from my lap. In her precise, neat hand, she completes the rest of the form, stopping only when she reaches the last page, the page that requires my signature.

"Okay, sweetie, just sign here and we're done," she says. I can't remember the last time she called me "sweetie." My entire insides swell up, pushing me to the brink of tears. She loves me. She really loves me.

I take the clipboard from Mom and sign the form.

And then we wait.

Finally, a slight man in glasses walks into the room and calls my name. Mom and I shuffle through the door and follow him down a narrow, poorly lit hallway into a narrow, poorly lit office. He takes a seat behind his desk and directs us to be seated as well.

"I'm Peter," he says. "I'm going to go over your form with you and make sure everything is in order before the judge signs it."

"You mean there's a chance that the judge won't grant the injunction?" I say, trying to disguise my hopefulness as concern.

"Well, only if you don't have a case," he says. "My job is to make sure that the evidence and statements you've provided are . . . adequate."

"Her case doesn't need to be screened, if that's what you're getting at," Mom says, shifting forward in her chair. "I've already spoken with Judge Rob Davis, of the second circuit, and he assured me that my daughter's situation clearly calls for an injunction. I'm sure you can see that we're not like most of your clients."

Peter leans toward Mom and places his slender hands on the desktop. His hands are small, even given his size, and his nails are squared and clean. Deliberately clean. By displaying his perfectly manicured hands, Peter seems to be signaling to Mom that they are on the same team.

"Humor me," he says, giving Mom a warm smile. "It's my job."

Mom smiles in return and settles back into her chair.

"Okay, Sabrina," he says, turning his attention to me. "There are three things a respondent, or stalker, has to have done in order for a judge to grant a stalking injunction. Firstly," he says, ticking the items off on his tiny, immaculate fingers, "the respondent has to have stalked you two or more times. Secondly, he should have known that the stalking would cause you to fear that you or a family member could be physically hurt or emotionally distressed. And thirdly, the stalking actually made you or an immediate family member emotionally distressed."

"Sabrina's situation clearly meets those criteria," Mom says.

"Good." Peter flips through my paperwork. "Looks like you've attached a sworn statement and a photograph of the respondent," he says. He continues to peruse the form, nodding his head occasionally. Then he knits his eyebrows together and looks up at me.

"Now here, Sabrina," he says, "under item number four, you've indicated that the stalking began at your place of employment. But you haven't attached any evidence of this. Did you report these incidents to anyone at your work?"

If I can answer this question correctly, I may be able to derail this whole stalking injunction business. Maybe it's possible that I can persuade Peter that there isn't enough evidence for my case against Calvin. Maybe it's possible that I can still come out of this thing unscathed.

"I did talk to security once," I say, "but they didn't write up a formal report or anything. And I don't think any of my coworkers actually ever saw the guy, you know, in action."

"Hmm," Peter says, clasping his hands together and resting his chin on his thumbs. "You may want to talk to security again, before you file, and see if they can get you a written statement. It would help your case."

I am tempted to lean across the desk and kiss Peter fully on the lips. But then Mom pipes in and ruins everything.

"I've already spoken to Judge Davis about that," Mom says. "He said that a statement from Sabrina's employer isn't necessary. The fact is, this man knows where Sabrina works, he knows where she lives, and he seems intent on harassing her. I'm certain my statement and the photo of the stalker in front of our home is evidence enough."

Peter's face flushes red. Mom is telling him how to do his job, but he keeps his mouth shut. He's obviously smart enough to realize that Mom is not the kind of person you want to get in a power struggle with.

"Alright then," he says, placing my form in a wire basket on the edge of his desk. "I will pass your paperwork onto the judge for signature."

"And then what?" I say.

"Well, then the respondent will be served the injunction, hopefully within the next day or two. As soon as it's served, the injunction will begin to protect you. The injunction orders the respondent to stay away from your work, home, and vehicle."

I still can't believe that this is really happening. How did I let things come to this? Tomorrow or the next day, an officer is going to show up at Calvin's home and serve him with papers. I can't even begin to imagine how he'll react to that. Calvin is something of a wildcard.

"What if the respondent doesn't obey the order?" I ask.

"Then you call the police," Peter says, "and the respondent can be arrested and charged with a crime."

This is too much. I suddenly feel like I am going to vomit.

"Sabrina, are you okay?" Peter asks.

"I don't know," I say. "This whole thing makes me really, really uncomfortable."

"You feel uncomfortable," Peter says, "because you're being stalked. Once the injunction is served and the respondent stops bothering you, you're going to start feeling a whole lot better."

Fat chance.

"There is one last thing," Peter says. "It's possible, once the injunction is served, that the respondent may choose to contest the case. If that happens, you will have to go to a hearing. I would suggest you get a sworn statement from your employer, just in case the respondent decides to fight this."

I nod and weakly stand. Mom thanks Peter for his time and then gently wraps her arm around me and leads me out of the office. I glance over my shoulder at my Request for Civil Stalking Injunction form on Peter's desk. The matter is now literally out of my hands. How did I let this get so completely out of my control?

Mom steers me down the hall toward the vending machines. She needs a Diet Coke. I lean against the wall as she rummages through her wallet for some change. She looks over at me and gives me a sympathetic smile. I relish this simple gesture of affection, certain it will be the last I receive for a long time. Tomorrow or the next day, the injunction will be served, and then this jig is up. Calvin will hate me. Mom will hate me. Dad will hate me.

Everyone will hate me.

My stomach lurches violently, and I keel over and throw up on the floor. Mom gasps and then races toward me, carefully sidestepping the mess I've made. She takes me to the women's room and helps me wash up.

"I'm disgusting," I say through hot tears.

"No you're not, sweetie," she says.

But I am.

We drive home in relative silence. Mom puts on her sunglasses and blasts Celine Dion. I stare straight in front of me. About a mile from home, we get stuck behind a truck that boasts the name Hale Plumbing on the rear.

"I wonder if that was intentional," Mom says, pointing to the tagline under the company name. There, in bold red letters, is the sentence,

"For all your plumbing needs, go to Hale."

It seems like an odd marketing strategy to essentially tell prospective customers to go to hell. Usually, I'd find this use of a homonym amusing. But not today. Frankly, I don't need the directive. I'm already there.

Chapter 26

Every action has an equal and opposite reaction. This is why, ever since I filed the stalking injunction, I have been bracing myself for the inevitable backlash. Only, by Friday night, a full day after taking action against Calvin, nothing's happened. I've done perhaps the worst thing in my entire life without consequence or repercussion. I'm beginning to think I'm some kind of Wonder Woman—impervious to the pesky cause-and-effect thing that plagues mere mortals.

Heather, however, seems intent on keeping me rooted in reality. Her opposite and equal response to having been called a mistake is to ignore me entirely. This behavior, of course, is not novel, but after the ground we've made the past few weeks, her indifference toward me especially stings. Even though we're seated at the same dinner table, Heather looks right through me. For a girl who flunked high school physics, Heather has a pretty good handle on Sir Newton's laws.

Mom's reverted back to her usual habit of overlooking me too. Now that the stalking injunction is presumably in effect, I guess Mom figures she no longer needs to, you know, nurture and protect me. She, Dad, and Heather are engaged in a lively discussion about whether or not Mack should have to meet Jordan Greene, aka the soon-to-be Wicked Stepmother. No one, apparently, cares if I have anything to contribute to the debate. I pick at the chicken cordon bleu on my plate, drawing out the toothpick in the center with my fork and skewering it through a broccoli stem.

"I don't see why this is any of your business," Heather says.

"It's my business," Mom says, "because Mack is my grandson, and he's a resident in my home."

She shoots and scores.

"Now Cindy . . . ," Dad says.

Mom, of course, goes for the block.

"Don, both you and I agree on this. If Jordan Greene is going to marry Thayne, then she's going to be a part of Mack's life. She's going to be a part of our lives, really, whether we like it or not."

"She is not going to be a part of my life," Heather says, slamming her water glass on the tabletop.

"Well then," says Mom, "if that's the case, then maybe I'll just have to call Thayne and arrange a time for Mack to meet Jordan myself."

"For what it's worth," I say, stepping onto the court, "I think Heather should be the one to decide if and when Mack meets Jordan."

I go for the assist, but Heather doesn't make the layup. In fact, she doesn't say anything at all. No one does. It's as if I haven't spoken at all.

I reach for the gravy boat and drown my uneaten chicken in a pool of soupy yellow sauce. Really, I'm trying to drown out the vision of my future, which extends before me like so many horrendous family dinners. I start to feel suffocated imagining the awful way I'll spend the rest of my life. Heather and Mom will continue to battle, Dad will continue to mediate, and I will continue to be, perpetually and systematically, ignored.

This vision has the principles of physics to back it up. After all, an object at rest tends to stay at rest.

"Sabrina," Mom says, waving a hand in my direction, "clear the table."

I stand and start collecting the dirtied silverware. On my way to the sink I nearly stumble over Mack, who is crouched on the floor, pushing his Matchbox cars around. Dad clears his plate from the table and then heads outside to check the mail. He soon returns, wagging a yellow postcard at me. My stomach hits the ground. I grab the postcard from his hand, fully expecting it to be another notification from Caltech. But, instead of Caltech's logo, I see a graphic of a smiling molar clutching a toothbrush. The postcard is merely a reminder of my upcoming appointment to have my cavity filled by Dr. Paul Nelson. It's a good thing too, because I'd nearly forgotten about my decaying tooth.

"That appointment might be a little awkward, don't you think?" Dad asks.

"Maybe," I say, running my tongue over my back molars. "But I might as well go. I hate walking around with imperfect teeth."

"Well, if that's the case, then you'd better keep the appointment," Dad says, planting a kiss on my forehead. "But as far as I'm concerned, you're perfect just the way you are."

I most definitely am not. I'd like to return Dad's smile but find I can't meet his eye. Instead I stash the postcard in my pocket and continue clearing the table. After I load the dishwasher I slump down on the ground next to Mack. We take turns rolling Matchbox cars across the floor, shoving them off with greater and greater force until they crash into the baseboards.

Late that night, when everyone's asleep, I lie in bed, wide awake. I reach for my phone and browse the headlines on BuzzFeed, stopping in incredulity at one that reads "Girl Forgives Shark That Bit Her."

Yeah, right.

I creep out of bed and wander down to the kitchen for a glass of milk. For good measure, I grab a couple of Oreos too, and then kick it old school and hunker down in front of the computer. I spend the next half hour or so aimlessly searching the web, bathed in the synthetic glow of the monitor. Really, I'm just trying to lull myself to sleep. Unfortunately, browsing the Internet isn't helping. First of all, there's the email from Caltech in my inbox, the one reminding me that the housing deposit is due at midnight. And then there's the status update on Calvin's Facebook page, the one that reads: *Payback's a real kick in the teeth.*

By virtue of this message, I assume he has been served with the stalking injunction. I read the message again and then spend an inordinate amount of time wondering whose payback he's referring to: mine or his.

I'd like to talk to somebody about what to do about the housing deposit. I'd like to talk to somebody about what to do about Calvin. By force of habit, I surf over to Cleverbot.com.

When the white dialogue box appears, I realize that it's been a while since I've visited the site. I should feel guilty for being so neglectful, but I don't. It's strange, but I can't say that I've missed our conversations.

Still, I begin with an apology.

—*Sorry we haven't talked in so long. I've been in Hale.*

—*Really? How was it?*

—*Horrible. Now everyone hates me.*

—*I don't hate you.*

Talking to Cleverbot isn't so bad. In fact, talking to Cleverbot may be better than talking to an actual living, breathing human being.

I type: *Have you ever been in pain?*

—*Yes, I am currently.*

—*What kind of pane?*

The blue cursor blinks at me as Cleverbot processes this question. Obviously, my use of a homonym has Cleverbot puzzled. It has me puzzled too. I don't know why I replaced "pain" with "pane." Maybe there's a part of me that wants to test Cleverbot. Maybe there's a part of me that knows that talking to this robot is much, much worse than talking to an actual living, breathing human being.

Finally, Cleverbot responds with: *From now on end every sentence with over. Over.*

Something inside me crumbles as I read this reply. Still, I give Cleverbot one last chance at redemption. I type: *I feel like I've opened a vane and am being bled dry. Over.*

I wait with bated breath for Cleverbot's response. The blue cursor flashes, and then: *A cow from the moon? You got wax in your eyes or something?*

I close the browser.

I rest my head in my hands and sit very still. An object at rest tends to stay at rest. And I'm not going anywhere. I stare at the computer monitor, defenseless against the negative thoughts that threaten to consume me.

And then I see it.

Out of the corner of my eye, I spy Dad's checkbook, resting on the edge of the desk beneath the reading glasses he wears when he's paying the bills. I pick up the book and thumb through it, taking special note of the blocky black numbers edging the bottom of each check.

An object at rest tends to stay at rest unless acted upon by an unbalanced force. The weight of that checkbook in my hand is definitely making me feel a bit unbalanced.

I pull up my email again and open the notice from Caltech. There's a link to the housing department in the body of the email, and after a few simple clicks of the mouse, I arrive at the page where I can make an online payment. I click on a drop-down menu and select the option to pay by check. A window opens with an image of a check with bright red arrows identifying the routing and checking numbers. It is too easy.

An object at rest tends to stay at rest. Unless . . .

Quickly, I enter the account information into the website and click on the green button to confirm the payment.

Chapter 27

In the morning, I leave home.

Not, you know, for good. At least, I'm not planning on leaving forever. It's just, after a miserable, sleepless night, I couldn't stand another minute in the place that is basically a crime scene. And crime scenes are made for fleeing. So first thing this morning I started up the Corolla and headed out of town. I was kind of hoping that the worries that are plaguing me would act like obedient dogs and stay put. But now, nearly fifty miles from home, they are still right behind me, nipping at my wheels.

I step on the gas. The lush green trees lining the highway are the only thing between me and the big, boundless sky. The windows are rolled down and the radio's turned up, and if I weren't feeling so hounded at the moment, this drive might actually be pleasant.

It might be pleasant, if it weren't for the fact that I am now officially both a liar and a thief.

If filing a stalking injunction isn't going to force a confession, then stealing $2,500 from my parents certainly will. I guess this is why, even though I am currently speeding away from home, this drive doesn't exactly feel like an escape. It's more like one last hurrah. One last taste of freedom, before I start serving time.

I'm cruising along the empty highway, the wind whipping my hair, when the seamless line of trees is suddenly interrupted by one of those classic yellow and brown signs from the Forest Service. On a whim, I take the turn-off and proceed down a dirt road toward the parking lot for the Wilderness Bird Refuge. I haven't been here since a field trip in sixth grade, and my only memory of that visit is of the soggy ham sandwich Mom packed for my lunch. So when I park the Corolla and step outside, I am completely stunned. The landscape I'm in is considerably more remarkable than lunch meat.

I sling my purse over my shoulder and lock the car, even though, other than my Corolla and a lone bicycle locked to a post, the parking lot is empty. I step onto the boardwalk and inhale the fresh morning air. Already, I'm finding the solitude refreshing.

I follow the boardwalk through a marshy field of reeds and hovering dragonflies. After a few hundred yards, the boardwalk gives way to a rocky trail that edges a glistening blue lake. It's cooler by the water, and I hug my arms around myself as I stumble along the trail, my flip-flops slapping the ground as I go. I am dressed in the knit shorts and tank top I wore to bed, and my hair is long and loose around my shoulders. This is one time when I desperately miss my Adventure Pal getup.

I stop at a clearing of aspens to catch my breath. The late morning sun is shimmering on the water and casting shadows in the woods. A lone bird soars across the blue canvas of sky, and I bring a hand to my brow to shield the sun's glare, trying to determine if it's an eagle or an osprey.

For a moment, I entirely forget about my thieving, lying ways. And then my phone rings.

I fish through my purse and find my phone. It's Mom. I can run, but I can't hide.

My ringing phone breaks through the stillness like shrill, abrasive birdsong. I briefly consider the possibility that Mom hasn't found me out—that she's just calling to check up on me, not to accuse me. I briefly consider the possibility that even if Mom has discovered the unauthorized transaction, she is capable of showing mercy.

I silence my phone and slip it back in my purse.

For a long time, I consider the possibility of staying here indefinitely, of receding into the forest and living off the grid. The prospect is strangely appealing, never mind the fact that I have next to no wilderness survival skills. Like it or not, I am going to have to go home and face what I've done. It's just the prospect of confessing my crimes to my parents is, like, the most unappealing thing I can think of.

I take leave of the cluster of aspens and start back on the trail. If I have to go home, I'm going to take the long way. I meander along the serene path, wholly absorbed in my own thoughts. When I've nearly completed the loop around the lake, I spot a flash of movement in the trees just ahead. My heart starts pounding, but before my imagination has a chance to run wild, a person emerges from the trees and joins me on the trail. Of course, after I take a second look at the man standing next to me, my heart starts pounding even harder.

"Joe?" I say.

The fact that I've run into Captain America in the middle of paradise is completely astonishing. Joe looks pretty surprised to see me too. He, however, recovers quickly and greets me with one of his dazzling smiles. Then he brings his index finger to his lips and grabs my hand. He pulls me into the trees he's just emerged from and leads me down a hill to the mouth of a small inlet. There in the water, standing on one long, reedy leg, is a very real and very pink flamingo.

Running into Joe took me by surprise, but spying a flamingo among the aspens and pines leaves me positively flabbergasted.

"Meet Pink Floyd," Joe whispers in my ear.

Pink Floyd is perhaps the most notorious bird in all of Boise. A few years ago, the zoo received a flock of Chilean flamingos. A keeper apparently forgot to clip the bird's wings, and one dark and stormy night it quite literally flew the coop. Since then rumors of Pink Floyd spottings circulate every once and awhile, but I've never actually believed that the flamingo had survived.

"You know that bird's here by complete accident, don't you?" I say.

"Yeah," Joe says, smiling at me. "I know."

I can't help but smile back at him. How strange that, of everyone I know, it is this gorgeous guy beside me that shares my interest in a fugitive flamingo.

"It looks kind of freakish," I say, studying the bird's exotic coloring. "You don't really expect to see a flamingo in Idaho."

"I think it looks beautiful," Joe says, leaning closer toward me, "in part because it's so unexpected."

"Yeah. But it doesn't exactly blend in."

"There's nothing wrong with standing out."

For a guy who's really into birds, Joe is spending an awful lot of time looking at me. I kind of wish I had actually taken the time to groom myself this morning. I turn toward Joe and meet his gaze, and he, suddenly shy, quickly shifts his eyes to the flamingo. We fall silent and, side by side, watch the flamingo until it spreads its black-tipped wings and gracefully flies away.

"Wow," Joe says, his voice still hushed. "I've been here all summer, but that was my first Pink Floyd sighting."

"You've been here all summer?" I say. "Really?"

"Yeah," Joe says. "For my thesis, I've been researching the relationship of migratory water birds with the lake's ecosystem. This particular ecosystem supports more than fifty species of birds, if you can believe it. I also participated in a larger study—that's how I've funded this whole adventure. That work was pretty tedious—it involved surveying certain points of the lake and taking a census of the birds. That study focused on the effect that the lake's water level has on bird use and habitats, although I'm really more interested in dietary matters."

It's the strangest thing to see Joe talk geek. I'm having a hard time getting my mind to assign the words he's saying to the mouth he's saying them with. This difficulty must be pretty transparent, because Joe suddenly stops talking.

"Sorry," Joe says, looking at the ground. "I have a tendency to ramble."

"No, I'm enjoying it. Really. It's just, all the ecology talk is a little . . . unexpected."

"Well," Joe says, blushing, "I guess today is a good day for surprises."

"I guess so."

"What are you doing here, Sabrina? You're not stalking me, are you?"

"No!" Now it's my turn to blush. "I recently adopted a strict no-stalking policy. I'm here because . . . because I needed to get away."

"It's a good place to get away to."

"Yeah. I just wish I had kind of, you know, dressed for the occasion. I pretty much just rolled out of bed this morning."

"I think you look incredible, Sabrina."

Guys like Joe aren't supposed to say girls like me look incredible. Then again, guys like Joe aren't supposed to pursue a graduate degree in ecology, or spend Saturday mornings here, at a wilderness preserve, bird watching. I'm not really supposed to be here today either. But I am. Maybe that's all that really matters.

"What are you doing here, Joe? I thought you were going back to Nebraska."

"I'm leaving tomorrow. I want to spend some time at home before fall semester starts. But I'll be passing through here again in a few weeks, on my way out to school." Joe fidgets with his hands, and then takes a deep breath. I wonder if he has any idea how good-looking he is. "If you're not busy, maybe we could get together then."

I am just about to dismiss my insecurities and take Joe's offer at face value. As improbable as it is, I'm pretty sure Captain America is asking me out. But then, my phone rings.

I pull my cell out of my purse and look at the screen. It's Mom.

"Sorry," I say, silencing the call. "You were saying?"

"I was saying," Joe says, "that I want to see you again."

This is the kind of line that, once dropped, is supposed to reel me in. And it almost works. I can feel myself being drawn toward Joe as if pulled by an invisible wire. Reflexively, I step forward and flash Joe a smile that is nearly as wide and warm as the one he is giving me.

I am just about to drop some kind of line of my own when my phone rings again. This time it's Dad. Without hesitating, I answer the call. Only, the voice on the other line doesn't belong to Dad. It belongs to Mom.

What can I say? She's good.

In a sharp tone, Mom demands that I explain why an officer just showed up at our door and served me a stalking injunction against one Brad Klein. Joe was right. Today is just a wonderful day for surprises.

Chapter 28

After the phone call, it takes me a minute to orient myself. I feel like I've suffered some kind of head injury, because I'm having trouble figuring out what I'm doing next to a beautiful lake with a cool Adonis, even though my life has just gone up in flames.

I look blankly at Joe and think about the lovely news I just got from Mom. Calvin has filed a stalking injunction. Against me.

Payback really is a kick in the teeth.

"Sabrina, is everything okay?"

"Yes," I lie. "Sorry. What were we talking about?"

"About getting together," Joe says.

"When?"

"In a few weeks," Joe says. "I'm going to be passing through Boise on my way out to school."

"I have no idea what I'll be doing in a few weeks," I say, in light of the fact that my future has suddenly become a gaping black hole.

"What about tonight, then?"

"Tonight? I can't tonight. Something's come up."

Joe shuffles his feet in the dirt. I wish I could explain things to him, but a thick mental fog has taken occupancy in my brain, obscuring any hope I have of finding a rational thought.

Maybe this explains the really stupid thing I do next. I don't ask Joe for his phone number or give him my own. I don't find out his last name or the name of school he attends. I don't do any of the things you should do when an unbelievably wonderful guy says he wants to see you again. Instead, I turn from Joe, scramble up the small hill to the trail, and start running toward the parking lot.

Yeah. I know.

I come home to find my parents huddled together on the front room sofa, Dad's arm draped protectively around Mom's shoulder, the pair of them staring at a document resting on the center of the coffee table. Their voices are paper thin and their bodies are bowed, and they seem, for the first time, old. They look like they are keeping vigil. They look like someone has died.

They stop whispering when I enter the room. Mom raises her head to glare at me, but Dad keeps his eyes fixed on his moldy oldies. I pause mid-step and wait for Dad to acknowledge me, to give me some sign that he still loves me.

Dad doesn't move.

On wooden legs, I walk to the coffee table and tentatively pick up the piece of paper. There should be no reason for my hesitancy. The document clearly belongs to me. My stomach performs an impossible gymnastics routine as I read that I am hereby ordered by the State of Idaho not to go within fifty feet of Brad Klein's residence, place of employment, and vehicle, for three years.

I can now add stalker to my rapidly growing list of vices.

"Explain," Mom says.

I purse my lips into a tight seal and glance at Dad's moldy oldies. The sight of those grass-stained Reeboks is positively heart-wrenching. A constricting lump forms in my throat. I can't say that I lied. I can't say that I'm not perfect.

"If you can't explain this," Mom says, "then maybe you can explain why someone used our checking account yesterday to make a rather large payment to Caltech."

"Mom," I plead. Sadly, this entreaty only adds fuel to Mom's rage. She slips out from under Dad's lifeless arm and marches toward me, positioning herself for a fight. I have half a mind to drop to my knees and beg for mercy. Even on my best day, I am no match for Mom. I turn to Dad, hopeful that he will step in and referee the inevitable bloodbath, but he is still slumped on the sofa, staring vacantly at the floor.

"What's going on, Sabrina?" Mom says.

I fight back tears and attempt to defend myself. I've told so many lies, but they've all centered on concealing one thing. I take a deep breath, and decide to tackle this monster head-on.

"I want to go to Caltech," I say.

"We don't always get what we want," Mom says. Her words are hard. Cold. Unyielding. They fall from her mouth and collect at my feet like ice cubes. I draw a sharp breath inward. We're just seconds into the argument, but already Mom's bested me. She's right. This isn't about Caltech at all.

"You don't want me," I say. This, of course, is the heart of the matter. This is the whole of my life, distilled to one salient, indisputable fact. "You never did."

"That's not true, Sabrina."

"Oh, come on, Mom. You can't say that having me wasn't a mistake."

"You were a surprise," Mom says. If she's trying to be reassuring, it's not working. She says "surprise" with the same hint of horror people use when they pair the word with heart attack or avalanche.

"I'm a mistake," I say, my voice uneven and loud. "That's why you don't want me to go to Caltech. It's just another inconvenience you didn't plan on."

"Sabrina, we've been over this already. It doesn't make sense to pay a dime for school when you can stay home and get a quality education for free."

"You paid for Tyler to go to an expensive school."

"And look how that turned out," Mom says.

"But I'm not like Tyler!"

"No," Mom says, her voice suddenly quiet. "You're not."

I flinch. Even though the words are spoken in a whisper, they are heavy with meaning.

"You don't want me to go to Caltech because you don't think I'm worth it."

"I don't want you to go to Caltech because it's not practical."

"It has the best biology program in the country."

"It's too expensive!"

"I'm not asking you to pay for it!"

"Aren't you?" Mom says. "Because that charge on our checking account suggests otherwise."

I wither under Mom's steely gaze. My scholarship covers the cost of tuition, but it doesn't pay for room and board. Room and board in Southern California, no less. Considering the fact that planning is perhaps my most highly esteemed virtue, it is almost comical that I haven't accounted for how I'll finance living out-of-state for four years.

Or have I? If I am being honest with myself, I have to admit that, in the back of my mind, I always assumed Mom and Dad would pony up the cash in the end.

"You paid for Tyler to go to an expensive school," I say again. It may be a lame argument, but it's the only one I have.

"That was nearly fifteen years ago," Mom says. "Back when Dad and I weren't staring retirement square in the face."

This comment reinforces everything I believe about my place in the world. My parents didn't plan on me in the beginning, and they haven't planned for me now.

"You still haven't explained why you were making a payment to Caltech," Mom says, "when you've already committed to go to Boise State."

"I didn't commit to Boise State," I say. There is no point in trying to cover up the truth anymore. Mom has already defeated me. "I accepted Caltech's offer instead."

"You accepted Caltech's offer," Mom says. "Did you hear that, Don? Sabrina thinks she's going to Caltech."

Dad lifts his head and locks eyes with Mom. He doesn't look at me.

"What was your plan, Sabrina? Did you think you could just run off to California without us noticing?"

"No."

"Well, then, what? School starts next month. What did you intend to do?"

I know exactly what I intended to do. That's the problem.

"I thought you'd let me go, if . . ."

"If what?"

"If you thought I wasn't safe here." My head jerks down toward the stalking injunction in my hand. The movement is slight and quick and possibly involuntary. It is a barely imperceptible action, but it is enough. I have given myself away.

"What does Brad Klein have to do with all of this?" Mom says, nodding at the injunction.

"I asked him to stalk me," I say.

"You what?"

"I asked him to stalk me," I say again. "I figured if you thought I had a stalker here, it might scare you into sending me to Caltech."

"You thought it would scare me?" Mom says, placing heavy emphasis on the concluding word. Like I said, she's good. She knows exactly who I was trying to scare. But the worst part is, he knows too. Bewildered, Dad turns to me like a weary traveler on a train platform, searching for a familiar face in the crowd. His eyes find mine, and I give a half-hearted wave of my hand, signaling to him that I am familiar, known. But he looks right through me, as if I, his own daughter, am a stranger.

Then his expression hardens. His eyes, suddenly absent of affection, are almost cruel.

"You're not going to Caltech, Sabrina," he says. "You're not going anywhere."

I hang my head and stare at Dad's Reeboks. Maybe it's just my imagination, but I swear that even the eyelets around the scraggly, sod-soaked laces close up to avoid my gaze.

· · · · · · ·

The days that follow are complete misery. I am allowed to work my scheduled shifts at the zoo, but other than that, I am under house arrest. I work, eat, sleep, and wallow in a seemingly endless pool of self-pity. It is easy enough to feel sorry for myself. Ever since my confession, I am no longer welcome in my own home. I tiptoe and skulk around, trying to dodge the contempt that lurks around every corner. Heather isn't speaking to me. My parents are, but only when it is absolutely necessary. Even though their behavior hurts, I don't blame my family for being angry. My lies made fools of each of them.

If my life were a movie, this would be the part where clips of me in varying states of depression are strung together by some sappy emo power ballad. But my life isn't a movie, and it doesn't come with a soundtrack or a fast-forward button. I have to endure these torturous days in real time, one excruciating minute after the next.

After Dad basically grounded me for life, Mom called the bank and reversed the payment to Caltech's housing department. Then she ordered me to clear up the whole stalking issue. I have not been terribly motivated to file the paperwork to contest the injunction. Despite the headache it's caused, being court ordered to stay away from Calvin feels strangely comforting.

So when he shows up at the zoo on Thursday, I keep my distance. I am stationed at the Elephant Encounter, detailing the differences between African and Asian elephants for an uninterested audience, when I catch Calvin out of the corner of my eye. He is seated on a bench by the west lawn, arms crossed, watching me. I try not to let his presence affect my performance, but my voice unwittingly slips into a higher register. When a red-headed girl in the crowd asks me a question, I can only answer with an absent stare.

As soon as I conclude my presentation with a half-hearted plug for conservation, Calvin rises from the bench and walks toward me with long, determined strides. When he's just about reached me, I stick out my arm and attempt to fend him off with an open, outstretched palm.

"The State of Idaho forbids you from coming within fifty feet of me," I say.

"Well, yeah," Calvin says, dismissing my handmade stop sign and breaching the space between us with one easy step. "But I could say the same thing about you."

Calvin laughs at me with his big, blue eyes and absently laces his fingers together. Something about those long, slender fingers strikes me as abnormal. I take in his gangly limbs and his almost excessive height, and wonder for a moment if he doesn't have Marfan's, that syndrome some historians suspect afflicted Abraham Lincoln. Calvin clearly possesses the disease's characteristic features—long, thin fingers, unusual height, a defective, utterly useless heart.

"Why did you file a stalking injunction against me?" I blurt out.

"Because," Calvin says, "I thought you posed a threat."

My mind flashes to the night Calvin so cavalierly

arrived at my house, and how Heather, looking impossibly beautiful, was waiting for him on the front step.

"The only thing I threatened was your social life!"

"I swear, Sabrina, I didn't think you'd find out about that."

"Heather's my sister! How was I not going to find out if the two of you hooked up?"

Calvin at least has the decency to try to look remorseful. His shoulders sag and his eyes droop down, away from me.

"I can't believe you were going to go out with her," I say. "You had to have known how much I liked you."

Calvin sheepishly meets my gaze in admission that he did, indeed, know how much I liked him.

"That's the only reason you paid any attention to me, isn't it? You were just using me to get to my sister."

"If anyone was being used, it was me," Calvin says. "Remember, the whole perv for hire thing?"

A crowd has started to form around us—a crowd that is considerably more engaged than the one I dismissed just moments earlier. I should take this burgeoning mob as a sign that I am making a scene. Instead, I stupidly keep going and transform a mild scene into a full-on spectacle.

"Then what was it, Calvin?" I shout. "Why didn't you want me?"

The volume of my voice can't disguise the vulnerability in my words. My audience leans forward, clearly eager for more of this impromptu melodrama. I instinctively pull at the brim of my safari hat, wishing I could melt into the concrete and vanish completely. Calvin himself looks uncomfortable, but he at least has the presence of mind to usher me off the pavilion and away from the gawking bystanders. He leads me to the lawn next to the Primate House and I sink into the shade of a towering Chinese elm. Calvin sits next to me and folds his long legs in front of him. I tug a piece of grass from the ground and begin to separate it in two with my fingernail. I'm waiting for Calvin to say something, but he seems content with the silence.

"Everything's ruined," I finally say. "My parents know about you. And Caltech. They, like, entirely hate me now."

"Your parents don't hate you."

"They do. I didn't just lie to them. I stole from them too. I used their checking account number to pay for housing at Caltech."

"So you're going?"

"No. My mom reversed the charge. The deadline for living in the residence halls has come and gone."

"You don't have to live on campus. I'm pretty sure they have apartments in Pasadena."

I shrug and pluck another blade of grass from the ground.

"All you'd have to do is look on Craigslist, find a roommate, and go."

"I can't afford to pay for an apartment."

"Then get a job."

"You don't get it, do you, Calvin? My parents won't let me go."

"Really? Because it seems to me like the only person keeping you here is you." Before I can protest this rather outrageous assertion, Calvin continues. "Sabrina, I know it's scary, but at some point or other, you've got to have the courage to live your own life."

"Geez, Calvin, what are you? A life coach?"

"I'm just trying to help."

"I don't need any help." My words sound hollow and false. "Besides, I don't deserve to go to Caltech. Not now. Not after everything I've done."

"No one expects you to be perfect, Sabrina."

"Don't they?"

"No." Calvin looks at me thoughtfully, stroking his beard with his spindly fingers. "Sometimes I think you never really wanted to go to Caltech. Sometimes I think this whole thing has just been a way for you to reinforce the narrative you've invented for yourself."

"What narrative?"

"The one that lets you use your parents' mistake as an excuse for not making any of your own."

I finger the dissected blade of grass in my hands and let Calvin's words take root in me. Maybe, just maybe, he's on to something.

"Sorry, Sabrina," Calvin says. "I'm being a tool. I didn't come here to lecture you."

"Then why did you come?"

"To apologize." He looks right at me when he says this, his face the very picture of contrition. "And to let you know that I'm going to revoke the stalking injunction I filed against you. Just in case you decide you want to see me sometime in the next three years."

"I don't know," I say. "It just might take me that long to forgive you."

"I hope not. Who knows? Maybe in three years, I'll have worked through my commitment issues."

"Maybe in three years I won't be such an emotional wreck."

"You won't be." Calvin takes a hold of my hand and gives it a tight squeeze. This vote of confidence is oddly reassuring. Calvin stands and pulls me up with him. When he releases my hand, I'm not sure I want him to let go.

"I guess I should get back to work," I say, although, really, work is the last thing on my mind.

"Okay." He gives me a wry grin that looks like good-bye. "You know, I've never met anyone like you, Sabrina."

"Me too," I say. He is staring at me with those big, blue eyes, smiling at me with those lips that hold the memory of my first kiss, and then he is walking away from me on those long, lean legs. He is walking away from me, and I am standing, alone, in the muted, dappled sunlight that is streaming through the leaves of the Chinese elm, part shadow, part luminance.

Chapter 29

Wednesday morning, I stumble into the kitchen to find Heather perched on the edge of a bar stool, mashing a soggy bowl of Wheaties with a spoon. It's early still, but she is already dressed, her auburn hair spilling down her back in loose, pretty curls. When she sees me she plunges the spoon into the cereal with a good deal of aggression and then pushes the bowl away from her. She still has not uttered a word to me since her near date with disaster. If it weren't directed toward me, I'd have to say this show of discipline is rather impressive.

I round the island and fill a glass with lukewarm tap water. I rest against the stove, facing Heather, and slowly sip the water. Heather sets her jaw into a hard, solid line. Other than the sound of cartoons trailing in from the family room, the kitchen is quiet. Eerily so. Like the calm before a storm.

Heather may not be ready to forgive me, but I'm ready to apologize. Only, I can't really say I'm sorry if she is determined to pretend that I don't exist. I plant my feet into the ground and bore into Heather with my eyes, challenging her to speak. The odds of winning this battle are in my favor. The only item on my day's agenda is (ugh) an afternoon dental appointment with Dr. Paul Nelson. Until that time, I'm willing to stand my ground and wait for Heather to acknowledge me.

Heather darts her eyes to the clock and then she seizes a paper napkin on the countertop and wrings it mercilessly in her hands. Slowly, but surely, I am breaking her down. I brace myself, waiting for the inevitable tongue-lashing I'm about to receive. But before Heather says a word, the chime of the doorbell breaks the sanctuary of our silence, and Heather stands on wobbly legs and starts toward the family room.

"Mackie," she calls, "they're here."

The house is a sudden flurry of activity. My entire family congregates around the front door, as if practicing some sort of emergency drill. Heather smooths Mack's wispy hair with her hand. Mom hands the baby off to Heather and Dad grants her an encouraging smile. I look on from the kitchen, mystified. When Heather gives Dad a slight nod of her head, he reaches for the handle and opens the door.

There, on the front step, are Thayne Stockett and Jordan Greene. The bold and the beautiful.

So it is this, and not my steely gaze, that explains Heather's caginess this morning. It is a testament to just how extreme my punishment has been that I had absolutely no idea that this horrifically exciting meeting was about to take place.

Even though I'm the only one caught off guard by the dynamic duo on the doorstep, it's clear that all of us are a little starstruck. Even Mom is tongue-tied. Jordan Greene may have grown up just a few blocks from here, but for the past few months, her face has graced the cover of every checkstand magazine. Even though hers is certain to be a fleeting fame, she plays the part of celebrity well. She tosses her blonde, flat-ironed hair and removes her movie star sunglasses with a practiced flick of her wrist. And it's crazy because for a moment I forget that she is here to meet her fiancé's ex-girlfriend's family. She demonstrates none of the anxiety you would expect from someone in her situation. Instead, it's as if she's just arrived at a press junket, and we are her admiring fans.

"Heather! It's been forever!" Jordan says, easily breezing through the tension-thick air. She gives Heather a quick hug, squishing Brodie in the process, and then steps back to get a better look at my sister. "You're so thin." This statement would normally be interpreted as a compliment. Heather, despite her still-soft belly, is, in fact, thin. But coming from Jordan, who is practically skeletal, the remark sounds insincere. Her legs and arms extend from her in thin, flat lines. She could easily be classified as two-dimensional.

"Thanks," Heather says, placing a self-conscious hand over her stomach.

"Well," Jordan says, turning to Thayne, who is still standing on the front porch, "aren't you going to introduce us?"

Thayne, always the typical jock, greets us by way of a quick chin nod. He takes a tentative step inside. Unlike Jordan, he's under no illusion that we are admiring fans.

"This, obviously, is Heather," he says. "Then we've got Don, Cindy, and . . ."

When his eyes fall on me, he stalls. Thayne was together with my sister for ten years, but it's possible that he is unaware of my existence. I'm not the kind of girl that registers on his radar.

"Sabrina," Heather says finally.

Thayne shrugs his shoulders and then turns his attention to Mack, who is hiding behind Dad's legs.

"And this big guy is Mack-Attack."

"Thayne!" Jordan gushes. "He's a mini you!"

Thayne gathers Mack up in his ropy arms and then tosses him recklessly high in the air. Mack is all smiles, clearly enjoying this show of attention.

"Why don't we have a seat?" Dad motions toward the front room. Everyone shuffles after him, but no one sits down. Instead we all stand awkwardly around the coffee table, stealing glances at each other and sharing a long, uncomfortable silence.

"Sounds like you're about to make a big commitment, Thayne," Dad says finally.

"Yep."

"You have to see my ring," Jordan says, thrusting her left hand toward us. Given the ginormous diamond she flashes at us, I'm surprised she can lift her hand at all. The diamond is perfect and shiny and huge, and, like everything else about Jordan, comes with a whiff of artificiality.

We politely ooh and ahh over the ring. And then we endure another round of uncomfortable silence.

"We should get going," Thayne says, nudging Jordan with his elbow.

"We're going to get Mack fitted for his tux," Jordan says. "He's going to be our little ring bearer."

"I can't imagine all the work it must take to plan a wedding," Heather says.

"It's insane," Jordan says. "And there's so much pressure to make it just perfect. You know, because of all the media coverage."

"Paparazzi," Thayne says wearily, as if dodging flashing cameras is a completely mundane activity. Then he swings his arm around Jordan, claiming her as his trophy, and grins an ugly jock grin at Heather. It strikes me that Thayne is still playing the same games he played in high school, only now he's playing on a bigger field. And it's painfully obvious at the moment who the winner is.

"How long do you plan on having Mack today?" Heather says, her voice brisk and businesslike. She is starting to look a little sketchy. Brodie has his slobbery hand wrapped around her hair, turning her pretty curls into a ratty mess. I can tell by the strained smile on her face that she is doing all she can to keep it together.

"Probably late afternoon. We have the fitting, and then," Thayne says, snatching Mack and tickling him until he doubles over with laughter, "we're going to take this guy to the movies and pump him up with sugar."

Mack stops giggling and gazes up at Thayne with adoring eyes. His expression is utterly heartbreaking. Thayne may be lavishing attention on Mack right now, but after the wedding, his involvement is certain to go back to the norm—a handful of visits a year, if that. Thayne may be ready to make a commitment to Jordan, but he never made one to Mack.

He never made one to Heather, either. I wonder if she is wishing he had. I wonder if she is longing to trade places with Jordan, to be the stunning starlet at his side, instead of the woman saddled with two kids and a lackluster future. A few weeks ago, I would have thought so. But now, I'm not so sure.

I do know for certain that when Heather walks Mack to the door and gives him a hug good-bye, I have never seen her exhibit such quiet strength. She stands in the doorway and clutches Brodie to her chest, letting her disheveled hair fall about him like a veil.

At this moment, I have never loved my sister more.

Chapter 30

Come afternoon, I pull myself away from the house of pain and arrive on time for my appointment with Dr. Paul Balding. Barb, the receptionist, greets me with a smug smile and a demand for my twenty-five dollar co-pay. Obviously, I no longer qualify for the family discount.

I stop by the Wall of Fame before taking a seat, searching for my own face among the dozens of others. It isn't there. I know it's absurd, but the absence of my picture on that wall fills me with a pang of sorrow. I crumple into a seat, staring at the perfect, cavity-free smiles before me, trying desperately not to cry. My picture is not on display anymore because I messed up. My picture is not on display anymore because I'm not perfect.

I study the mosaic of freckles and cowlicks, braids and braces, until it hits me: maybe my picture is not on display because I'm not a child anymore.

I'm not a child anymore. This thought is at once exhilarating and terrifying. I'm not a child anymore. So why have I been acting like one?

The thought that Calvin planted in my mind has started to bloom. Maybe I have been using my parents' mistake as an excuse for not making any of my own. If I am being honest with myself, I have to admit that the idea of going to Caltech scares me. And it's not just the whole living-away-from-home thing that's scary. The part about being accountable for my own decisions is pretty scary too. Because what if going away to school doesn't work out? What if it ends up being a mistake?

Everything inside of me screams that mistakes are one thing I can't afford to make.

But the thing is, I've already made mistakes. Lots of them. In fact, since my last trip to this office, not more than three weeks ago, I've made more mistakes than I care to recall. So what does that say about me?

Thankfully, a hygienist calls my name and rescues me from myself. I follow her into an examination room and hoist myself into the dental chair. I drum my fingers on the armrest and run my tongue over my decaying molar. Finally, Paul appears in the doorway, announcing his presence by loudly clearing his throat. He stands there for a moment, hesitating, buying time by fiddling with the clipboard in his hand. Clearly, he is uncomfortable. I had considered not keeping this appointment for my sake, but now I wonder if I should have canceled for Paul's.

"Sabrina," he says, forcing his way across the threshold of the doorway. "How are you?"

"Fine," I say, declining to elaborate. I'm not really in the mood to chat it up with Paul. He stands stiffly in front of me, clinging to the clipboard as if it's a security blanket. I'm guessing he's waiting for me to reciprocate with a question of my own, but I don't need to ask Paul how he is. It's obvious that he is not doing well. He has dark circles under his eyes and beneath the awful fluorescent lighting, his skin looks pitted and flawed, like pumice stone. After a strained silence, he sits on the rolling stool and scoots toward me. He tightens his hold on the clipboard, his knuckles turning bone white, and then clears his throat again.

"How's, um, Heather doing?"

"She's great," I say. "She started cashiering at a boutique downtown and ended up doing the cover art for their fall catalogue. She's, like, a really fantastic artist."

"I didn't know that."

"There's a lot you don't know about Heather."

"I'd say," Paul says.

If it were any other day, I'd let this response slide. After all, given the way things ended between my sister and Paul, his snarkiness is probably warranted. But I've already seen Heather wounded by one guy today. I'm not about to let her take another blow without putting up a fight.

"She made a mistake." Okay, Heather made a lot of mistakes, but who's counting? "She should have told you about her past, but who cares? It doesn't change who she is."

"I don't know." Paul pathetically slumps his shoulders. "I thought she was . . ." His voice trails off and he stares vacantly ahead of him.

"You thought she was what?"

"Perfect."

I think back to earlier today and the way Heather behaved with such dignity and grace. Then I look at Paul and his balding head and I start to get angry. I mean, he may have made Heather happy, but she made him happy too. Is he really about to sacrifice all that joy because Heather's not perfect?

"You don't have to be perfect to be loved." The words

cling to my dry throat like cotton balls. This sentiment, of course, isn't new, but finally, I believe it.

I don't have to be perfect to be loved.

I push the tray of instruments out of my way and slide out of the dental chair. My cavity doesn't need to be filled today. I can live with some imperfection.

"What you don't know about Heather," I say, "is that she's amazing. She's fun and creative and a great listener. She's a good mom. And she likes you, of all people.

"If anything, you're not good enough for her."

Before Paul can say another word, I turn on my heel and walk out of the room. I rush past Barb the receptionist and the Wall of Fame and push my way outside, trading the stale, antiseptic air of the office for the smothering heat rising off the parking lot. Inside my Corolla it is positively stifling, but even still a broad smile widens my face. What just occurred in that dentist office may very well qualify as my finest moment.

I pull out of the parking lot and head home. When I stop for the light at the intersection, I notice a black Lexus behind me. I also notice the driver. Paul catches me staring at him in the rearview mirror and gives me a curt nod. Heaven help me. I think I'm being followed.

Paul, indeed, is following me. In fact, he follows me all the way home. He parks his car alongside the curb and crosses the driveway toward me.

"I need to talk to Heather," he says, as if his presence needs an explanation.

I nod and then walk up the porch stairs and swing the front door open. Paul pads behind me in his navy blue Crocs. The house is cool and quiet. I lean on the banister and yell up the stairs for Heather. Of course, she doesn't respond. I yell for her again, louder this time.

Nothing.

Then Paul calls her name. This is when I know Paul has already forgiven Heather. His voice is filled with so much yearning that even I start to ache. He is suddenly vulnerable, standing at the foot of the stairs, his balding head gleaming in the sunlight. Paul's obviously aware that Heather may not respond to his call, either. His hands are trembling and his face has drained white, but he keeps his feet planted firmly on the ground. It strikes me that this is the kind of courage that adulthood demands. The courage to look foolish. The courage to admit fault.

The courage to lose.

After a moment heavy with waiting, Heather appears at the top of the stairs.

"Heather." When Paul says my sister's name again, she lights up. He's glowing too. By the time she's made her way down the stairs, there is so much illumination going on I nearly have to squint.

If either of them is aware that I am still in the room, they don't show it. I wonder at the way the world can at once be reduced to just two people, but at the same time feel so wonderfully magnified.

"Paul." My sister's voice is filled with so much tenderness that it feels like the entire room has just been swaddled in down.

This is when I know Heather has forgiven Paul too.

· · · · · · ·

Paul ends up staying for dinner. Needless to say, his presence at the dinner table leaves Mom suffering from a slight buzz. She's not the only one acting like she's under the influence of mood-enhancing drugs. The house is positively humming with happiness. There is the sense that things have been restored to order. Mack has returned from his compulsory outing with Ken and Barbie and is no worse for wear. Mom is dishing up the ingredients for Hawaiian haystacks and firing off orders at Dad, who is only too willing to oblige her. Heather is bouncing Brodie on her hip and wearing a perma-smile. She's still not talking to me, but she's not glaring at me, either.

When dinner's ready, we crowd around the kitchen island and load our plates with a mountain of sticky white rice and chicken gravy. Tentative hands reach for bowls of diced tomatoes, green onions, olives, and shredded cheese. I step back from the chaos and watch the ritual that is family dinner. It is a ritual that, if I decide to leave home, I won't participate in anymore. Even though I'm still here, I already feel the pain of missing. And there are so many things to miss: the sight of Dad at the counter, sorting the mail; the sound of Mom's high heels on the hardwood floor, certain and sure; the smell of baking bread and savory onions, announcing a home-cooked meal.

It would be so comfortable to stay here forever, to shelter myself in this cocoon of familiarity.

"Sabrina," Mom says, beckoning to me, "come on and dish up."

I turn to look at Mom. How is it that I have seen her face a thousand times but have never noticed how beautiful she is? How is it that every time she's said my name I've mistook the affection in her voice as annoyance? How is it that I've never realized that all Mom wants is for me to be as strong and self-assured as she is?

I start for the counter, but pause mid-step. Mom would want me to be brave. If I decide to stay home, I'm a coward.

"Sabrina," Mom says again, "dish up."

I muster all the courage I possess and stand my ground. I have made up my mind. I'm going to Caltech.

Chapter 31

That night I get to work. If I am really going to go to Caltech, I need a plan. A plan that, preferably, doesn't rely on fake stalkers or lies. My goal is to secure housing and land a part-time job before I tell my parents I've decided to leave home.

The clock on the computer monitor reads just after ten. By my estimation, I should easily be able to find an apartment and post my resume online before midnight.

Despite Calvin's advice, I bypass Craigslist and head for Apartmentfinder.com. The pro of splitting rent with another person is greatly outweighed by the con of that person being the next Craigslist killer. I am heartened when my search for apartments in Pasadena yields five hundred results. I scan the photos of pristine apartment buildings complete with palm trees and sparkling blue pools. Then I see the astronomical rates listed beside them. Instantly, I surf over to Craigslist. Maybe rooming with a potential murderer isn't such a bad idea after all.

Only, the rooms advertised on Craigslist aren't all that cheap, either. Given the fact that I currently have a measly $1,200 in my checking account, I need my monthly rent payment to be as small as possible. I randomly click on the ads, avoiding those that require a credit check (I have no credit) and steering towards those seeking a tenant that is "sober" and a "non-smoker." Most of the ads have a photo of the room, but the images are dark and grainy and not particularly helpful. What would be helpful is a photo of the prospective roommate. Skip the real estate and give me a headshot already.

Midnight comes and goes. At a quarter to one, I find a room advertised at an unbelievable $99 per month. I'm obviously suffering from sleep deprivation, because I actually click on the ad. The attached photo shows an unfurnished room complete with stained carpet and torn drapes. It is beyond sketchy. Try as I might, I simply can't imagine living in a place like this. I'd be safer picking up a hitchhiker than renting a room in Pasadena for 99 bucks a month.

It's one o'clock in the morning and I have next to no leads for housing and am not even close to finding a job. Coming up with a real, legitimate solution for my problem is much harder than I expected. As night creeps toward dawn, my mind starts drifting toward those easy, fantasy solutions again. Like, maybe I could go freegan and sustain myself by Dumpster diving. Or, I could pull a Rudy and claim squatter's rights on a janitor's closet on campus. Or maybe some distant relative will suddenly keel over and leave me an unexpected inheritance.

I take a deep breath. I don't have to figure everything out right now. I have plenty of time to come up with a plan.

To reassure myself, I look at the calendar. Classes at Caltech begin on August 20th. Today is (technically) the 7th. If I plan on making it to Pasadena by the first day of classes, I have fourteen days.

Fourteen days.

Two weeks.

One fortnight.

In other words, no time at all.

. . . .

The next day at work my brain is fried. I take my break at the Oasis, crunching popcorn and peanuts underfoot, and try not to let the cotton candy–scented air make me physically ill. I tug my safari hat down and hold my head in my hands. I want nothing more than a few minutes of complete silence.

Michelle, of course, wants to gab. She plops down beside me on the bench, rips into a bag of Fritos, and starts into a story straight from the Mommy Diaries. Apparently, last night her son stuck a Lego so far up his nose that she had to rush him to the emergency room. As far as Michelle's stories go, this one is actually pretty amusing, but the only response I can muster is a courtesy smile.

Michelle's fairly oblivious to social cues, but I must look really dejected because she abruptly stops talking and puts her hand on my shoulder.

"Are you okay today, Sabrina?"

I turn my red-rimmed eyes to Michelle. It's been a while since I've had someone to talk to. I take a deep breath and then start unloading my story on Michelle, who hangs on to my every word. When I finish her mouth is open so wide I'm afraid her jaw has literally come unhinged.

"You mean, you're planning on going to Caltech in two

weeks, and you don't have housing or a job?"

"I know. I'm an idiot."

Michelle doesn't argue this point.

"What about financial aid?"

"You had to apply in the spring."

"Why didn't you apply?"

I shrug my shoulders. Financial aid is just one of the many things I thought would be taken care of for me.

Michelle is quiet. Call me crazy, but for half a second, I think that discussing my predicament with Michelle might have actually been productive. And then, she reverts back to the Chronicles of Michelle.

"I have an aunt in Arcadia. She has a real pretty house. And she lives alone."

"Thank you, Queen of Random."

"Arcadia's only ten minutes or so from Pasadena. You know," Michelle arches an eyebrow at me, "she probably wouldn't mind if you stayed with her for a while—until you have time to find something more permanent."

This I did not see coming. The smile I give Michelle qualifies as far more than courteous. Maybe, just maybe, I'll be able to pull this thing off after all.

· · · · · · · ·

That night, Michelle sends me a Facebook message. In typical Michelle fashion, she leads with an invitation to dinner on Friday, and then, as if it's an afterthought, adds that her aunt would love a (temporary) roommate. Now that I have housing (temporarily) covered, I commence the job search. I polish my resume and post it to several employment websites and contact representatives at all of the major temp agencies in Pasadena.

A few days pass. I have a lot of lines in the hiring pool, but no one's biting. I go into my bank to see about the possibility of getting some kind of loan, just in case. The very nice loan officer at the bank very nicely informs me that, without a cosigner, the only money she can offer me is a credit card with a $500 line of credit.

Time is passing much too quickly. It's already T minus one week and I don't have any job prospects. I remind myself that finding a job, any job, isn't impossible. Surely, people have done more difficult things than this. I am capable of doing difficult things.

Maybe.

Friday night a beat-up minivan with a bumper sticker that says "Soccer is Life" pulls into our driveway. Michelle is here for our girls' night out. Even though I am technically still under house arrest, I couldn't refuse her invitation. I owe her big time for solving my housing problem. But before I can collect my purse and slip out of the house unnoticed, Michelle is out of the van and on the front porch. Dad peeks his head into the entryway as I open the front door. He eyes Michelle's denim capris and Teva sandals and gives her a reserved smile.

"Can I help you?" he says.

"Dad," I say, "this is my friend Michelle."

"This is Michelle?" Dad looks her over again.

"Guilty as charged," Michelle says.

"Well, hello." Dad's gaze drifts to the minivan parked in

the driveway before he extends his hand to Michelle. "It's a pleasure to finally meet you."

"I just love this daughter of yours," she says, taking Dad's hand in hers and giving it an energetic pump. "Sabrina and I have had an absolute blast working together this summer."

"Have you?" Dad raises his eyebrow at me and then turns back to Michelle. "Would you like to come in?"

Michelle consults her watch and shakes her head. "Better not. My husband will pitch a fit if I'm not home by eight. Our five-year-old insists that I put him down for bed. He's going through one of those fun phases."

"I've been there," Dad says. His eyes dart from Michelle to me. "Where exactly are you going, Sabrina?"

Michelle, of course, answers for me. "I'm going to snag Sabrina and take her out for sushi."

"Sushi?" Dad narrows his eyes at me and I in response make mine as wide and guileless as possible.

"It's okay if she comes, right?" Michelle says, picking up on our silent negotiation.

Dad takes in the denim capris and dirty minivan and caves. "Yeah, it's okay."

"Thank you, Dad." I grab Michelle by the arm and escort her to the minivan before Dad can change his mind. I open the passenger door and move a half-empty bag of Baked Lays from the seat to the console before climbing in. Michelle starts up the minivan and then reaches into the bag and starts munching. She has something of a chip addiction.

"Here," she says, reaching beneath the console and

plopping a massive CD case on my lap. "You choose the tunes."

"This is quite the collection," I say, flipping through the case. I don't want to think about how old she is. I mean, not only does she drive a minivan, she still listens to CDs.

"*Appetite for Destruction?*" I say, spying a Guns N' Roses album cover. "Michelle, I had no idea you were into hair bands."

"I'm not into hair bands."

"Um, Guns N' Roses? Van Halen? Bon Jovi?"

She smiles and grabs another handful of potato chips. I slide "Livin' on a Prayer" out of the case and pop it into the CD player.

The song begins. After a quite stirring intro, Michelle sings along. "*Tommy used to work on the docks . . .*"

I all but roll my eyes at her. "You're really into hair bands."

"Sue me." Michelle turns on her blinker as she merges onto the expressway. "I talked to Aunt Judy today. She's really looking forward to having you come stay with her."

"Me too."

"How's the job search going?"

I shrug and grab a handful of Baked Lays. I look out the window and listen to Bon Jovi belt it out. "*Woah, we're halfway there . . . Woah! Living on a prayer.*" Michelle has stopped singing along. She reaches across the console and squeezes my hand.

"Heaven knows I've been in my share of tight spaces, Sabrina. Usually I'm just sneaking by on faith, Frito Lays, and elbow grease. But life has a way of working itself out."

She removes her hand from mine and places it back on the steering wheel. "You'll find a job."

"I hope so." I push the back button on the player panel. "Let's listen to this one again."

"Look who's into hair bands now." Michelle turns the volume up and this time I sing along too. When in Rome and all that.

I need two things before next Friday: housing and a job. Thanks to Michelle, I have one. Let's hope faith, Frito Lay, and elbow grease take me the rest of the way.

Chapter 32

The next morning I grab a bag of Fritos from the kitchen cupboard, throw on my safari hat, and hunker down. If I'm going to find a job, I, Frito Bandito, am going to have to get aggressive. Immediately, I search the Internet for pet-related businesses in Pasadena and the surrounding areas. Turns out, the good folks in Pasadena like them some animals. My search yields results for businesses specializing in pet boarding, pet supplies, pet grooming, pet training, pet day care, pet therapy, pet sitting, and pet finders. There are veterinarians and clinics and animal shelters. I even come across a company that specializes in dolphin rentals for parties.

I compile a list of each company's name, address, and phone number. Then, I pimp my resume. Who knew so many skills could be derived from a summer job as an Adventure Pal? I am at once an expert animal handler, conservation specialist, and educator. Once my resume has been sufficiently beefed up and my family is well out of earshot, I initiate the cold calling.

The first few calls I make are a complete disaster. It takes me nearly ten attempts to figure out I should ask to speak to a manager. It takes ten more for me to nail down a sales pitch. Over the course of the next two days, I make nearly one hundred phone calls.

No one wants to hire me.

The rejections are completely demoralizing. I am just about to concede defeat when, late Wednesday afternoon, my cell phone rings. I answer to a Dr. Linda Manning, the director of an after-hours animal clinic in Pasadena. She says she is responding to the message I left for her regarding a possible job opportunity. She says she admires my pluck. She says she is a Caltech alum, that she also studied biology as an undergrad, that she would love nothing more than to help advance the career of another woman in the sciences.

Dr. Linda Manning offers me a job working the reception desk nights and weekends. She says the shift tends to be slow, and that I may just have to pass the time by studying for my classes.

I have known Dr. Linda Manning for all of ten minutes, and already I am completely and utterly devoted to her.

When I hang up the phone my whole body is shaking. I sit at the computer and create a document that details my housing and employment arrangements, as well as a breakdown of the estimated cost of living. I print out my plan and then, for good measure, I slip it into a manila folder. I'd like some time to compose a speech to accompany the document in said folder, but Mom returns home from work before I can even come up with an opening line.

"What's this?" Mom says. Before I can stop her, Mom snatches the folder and greedily consumes its contents with her eyes.

I suppose now is as good a time as any to drop the bomb.

"This is how I intend on supporting myself while I attend Caltech."

"Sabrina, do you really think you can work part time and still make the grades to keep your scholarship?"

"I don't know," I say. "But you got your real estate license while raising three kids and running a household. I don't see why this is any harder."

Mom cocks her head to one side and stares at me. She is sizing me up, measuring me. Then she turns her attention to the document in her hands. I can tell by her furrowed brow that she is measuring that too. Finally, she flips the folder shut and sighs in resignation.

"You already know the reasons I think going to Caltech is a bad idea," Mom says. "But, you're an adult now. If you're set on leaving, I can't make you stay."

When Mom hands the folder back to me, I finally feel like we are standing on equal ground.

· · · · · · ·

When Dad comes home from work a few hours later, he doesn't come inside. I peek out the front room window and see him sitting on the porch step, elbows on knees, head in hands. He looks seriously dejected. Mom creeps up behind me, aproned and whisking a bowl of instant pudding.

"He knows," she says. "I called him at work this afternoon. I wanted him to have some time to process the news."

He knows I'm leaving. Facing Mom was difficult, but this is heart-wrenching. I fortify myself with the manila folder and join Dad outside. The only movement he makes when I sit beside him is to wipe his brow, which is prickled with perspiration. It's hot, even in the shade of the porch eave. I don't know how to breach the silence, so instead I stare at my feet and then shift my gaze to the row of thirsty-looking marigolds lining the flower bed.

Finally, Dad lifts his head. He clears his throat but when he begins to speak his voice still sounds husky.

"We need to talk about this nonsense," he says.

I swallow hard and then hand him the spreadsheet from the manila folder.

"Not Caltech," he says, gently placing the paper on the porch step. "This *accident* nonsense."

"Oh," I say. This is unexpected.

"I still remember the day your mother told me she was expecting you. To be frank, initially that news was surprising. Your mother and I had given up on having another baby. It took some time for us to get used to the idea of having a newborn again. We had to reimagine our lives, and that can be . . . uncomfortable."

I nod. Dad wipes his brow again with the back of his hand. How I love those sure and steady hands.

"Turns out, there's an advantage to having a baby in your forties," he continues. "You're old enough to know how to enjoy it. Don't get me wrong—I enjoyed your brother and sister when they were little. But there were so many demands on your mother and me back then. Our wallets—and patience—were strained. But when you came along Sabrina, it was different. I had time to appreciate every stage of your childhood. And I did. Having you in my life has been an extraordinary gift."

Dad cups my face in his hands and plants a kiss on my forehead. Then he picks up the cost-of-living document and this time inspects it closely.

"Tell me what I'm looking at here," he says.

"This column lists my estimated expenses," I say, pointing to the paper. "And this over here lists my estimated income."

"Your mother said you found a job in Pasadena? At a veterinary clinic?"

"Yes."

"And school starts when?"

"Next week."

"Next week?" Dad looks like he's been punched in the gut. He takes a beat to recover by reviewing the paper in his hand again. "This is really sharp," he finally says.

"It's just a spreadsheet." There are more important things to be said. "Dad, I love you."

"I love you too, Sabby-apple." He looks at me for a long moment. "I wish you didn't have to go."

"Oh, Dad." I feel like I am going to cry. Thankfully, Mom opens the front door and prevents a downpour.

"Everything okay out here?" Mom says, joining us on the porch.

I turn to her and nod. Maybe everything's not okay at this exact moment, but I have confidence it will be.

"Good. Dinner's ready."

Dad puts his hands on his knees and slowly pushes himself up. He stands next to Mom and leans heavily into her.

"Our baby girl's leaving us, Cindy."

"I know it, Don." Mom puts her arm around Dad. He

gives me a beautiful, sad smile before Mom ushers him inside. Heart-wrenching is an understatement.

Chapter 33

The night before I leave for California, Paul throws me a farewell party at his house. Since I basically got him and Heather back together, I guess he figures he owes me. Spending my final night in Boise with my dentist isn't ideal, but I'm not complaining. I could really use a night off. Thankfully, I haven't had to prepare for the move all by myself. Mom has been surprisingly helpful. After she recovered from the initial shock of my imminent departure, she called the office and cleared her schedule for the week. Then she called the airline and booked herself a one-way ticket from Los Angeles to Boise. She said that even adults are better off making a long-distance drive with a companion.

Paul's in the kitchen, getting a tutorial on veggie chopping from Mom, and Dad and Heather are in the living room, doing their best to entertain the kids. I slip out the French doors that lead to the deck and enjoy a moment of solitude. The view is stunning, but instead of enjoying the moment, I start running over my checklist of things to do. I've packed my pitiful wardrobe into two suitcases. I've filled the Corolla with gas and had the oil changed. I've mapped out the route from home to Arcadia.

Everything has been taken care of. Even still, when Heather joins me outside, my heart starts pounding. I've taken care of everything except, you know, the really important thing. This is my chance to apologize for the whole name-calling incident. Only, I haven't spoken to Heather for so long, I'm not sure I remember how.

Thankfully, Heather decides to end her marathon silent treatment and speaks first.

"Paul told me what you said about me in his office."

"I'm sorry," I say. "About the other thing I said."

"I know." She leans against the slatted wood railing and rests her elbows on the banister. The evening sun streaks her auburn hair gold. The expression on her face is just as lovely. "I wouldn't have hit on Brad if I had known you two were . . . involved."

"I know."

Heather tilts her head toward me and grins. "I still can't believe you got mixed up with Brad Klein. Talk about an education."

"It was more like a complete failure."

"There's nothing wrong with failure," Heather says, "as long as you get it right eventually."

She peers inside at Paul, who is finishing up his culinary lesson with Mom. Paul must feel the weight of her gaze, because he suddenly lifts his head and looks in our direction. When he catches sight of Heather, his mouth drops open, as if she has literally taken his breath away. I don't doubt she has, what with the way the sun has nearly transformed her auburn hair to flames.

"Is it completely crazy that I think I'm in love with that man?"

"It's not crazy," I say. "It's obvious."

Paul beckons us inside. He's really outdone himself this time. There's not a Styrofoam container or take-out bag in sight. Instead, the table is covered in a linen cloth and bedecked with grilled chicken, orange rolls, and a colorful garden salad.

Paul, who is wearing an apron and toting Brodie on one hip, strikes me as terribly domestic.

"Geez, Paul," I say. "When did you become Martha Stewart?"

"I'm just trying to make up for last time."

He looks sheepishly at Heather, who in turn smiles and places a possessive hand on his arm. While these two are lost in a moment, the rest of us take a seat at the table. Finally, Paul pulls himself away from Heather and raises a sweating glass of ice water.

"To Sabrina," Paul says.

Everyone lifts their glasses to the center of the table and clangs them together. Everyone, that is, but Dad. The reality of my departure is taking a toll on his mood. He sits stiffly in his chair and concentrates on the untouched plate of food in front of him. I manage to eat, even though anxiety is tying my stomach in knots. I'm starting to worry that I won't be able to leave home without some sign from Dad that he is going to be okay.

After dinner, I help Paul clear the table. Dad remains seated. Paul is asking me questions about my travel plans, questions that suddenly strike me as trivial. I do my best to answer Paul, but I'm distracted by the sight of Dad, who apparently has gone comatose.

When the dishes are done, Mom produces a giant cake from Costco with "Good Luck, Sabrina!" written across the top in frosted cursive script. She sets it on the kitchen counter and begins to carve it into generous squares. Mack sees the cake and instantly starts into a tuneless version of "Happy Birthday." Heather and Mom indulge him and join in. Of course, when they finish, Mack demands an encore.

As they start into the song again, my knees buckle beneath me. I am leaving. Tomorrow. I grip the counter to steady myself as the reality of what I'm about to do settles over me. I might just pass out. Or worse, vomit all over the enormous cake.

Suddenly, Dad stands from the table. I fear for a minute that he is going to walk out of the room. But he doesn't leave. Instead, he stands beside me at the counter and starts to sing too. When he sings "Happy Birthday, Sabrina," his voice breaks. I bury my head in his chest and start to cry.

Dad wraps his arms around me and holds me like he did when I was a little girl. And then something kind of remarkable happens. Mom and Heather throw their arms around me too. The boys circle around us, reinforcing the tower of our legs. My knees are weak but, remarkably, I am still able to stand. I may be leaving home in the morning, but for now I am held up by this nation of arms and hearts and smiles.

No matter where life takes me, this is one place I'll always belong.

Chapter 34

Caltech is, simply, glorious.

I can't decide what feature of the campus thrills me more: the contrast of the pristine white buildings against the manicured green lawns; the elegant Athenaeum Rooms bedecked with chandeliers and gold-trimmed ceilings; the arched porticos beside lush koi ponds.

The hushed library with its winding, burdened stacks, the book spines beckoning to be opened like so many windows and doors.

The palm trees.

I feel like I am lost in some exotic academic paradise. Even Mom was dazzled by the campus. When we first wandered around the grounds, awestruck, she must have dropped the word "prestigious" a hundred times. Before she boarded the plane for Boise, she had already convinced Dad to bring everyone out for a visit during Christmas break.

If I had switched tactics and focused simply on the school's cache, I could have persuaded Mom to let me attend Caltech months ago.

Once school starts, I discover that the buildings on campus aren't the only thing I'm dazzled by. What goes on inside those buildings is pretty impressive too. I am enrolled in chemistry, molecular biology, writing, and calculus II. I voluntarily attend seminars with titles like "Captivated by Critters: Humans Are Wired to Respond to Animals" and "String Theory." The coursework is rigorous and completely invigorating. I lose myself in diagramming molecules and solving equations. I've missed the kind of problems that have clear, identifiable solutions.

Time would be better measured by the number of changes we make rather than the number of days we pass through. Because one week cannot possibly account for the time I've spent away from home. I have a new home, a new school, a new job, and possibly a new friend. Karen, a girl in my chemistry class, actually asked me to study with her tomorrow. She is a beautiful Korean with sleek black hair and extended eyelashes, and a complete nerd at heart.

Saturday morning I work an early shift at the Pasadena Pet Clinic. Dr. Linda Manning was right—the job is pretty underwhelming. Still, after a few hours of phone answering and light filing I'm grateful when my shift is over. I've been in California for a whole week and have yet to see the ocean. My feet are itching to feel some sand beneath them.

But first, I have to get past my landlady.

Aunt Judy is relaxing on the covered porch when I return from work. Her home in Arcadia is a white stucco rambler with a lovely red roof. I park my car in the driveway and walk toward her, passing through a tropical garden of hibiscus, gardenias, and (sigh) palm trees. Judy motions to a covered wicker chair and I follow orders and sit down beside her.

Judy definitely shares blood with Michelle. She has Michelle's same dark wavy hair and boxy figure. But they have more than just the physical in common. I mean, this woman can talk. Now I know where Michelle gets her gift of gab.

"How was work?" Judy asks.

"Slow," I say, "but fine. I got in some good studying."

"That's nice. You know, when I was in college, I worked at a little pizza parlor . . ."

And she's off. I let Judy's words wash over me and breathe in the soft, humid air. I don't have a problem listening to her stories. It's a small price to pay for her generosity.

Just before Judy arrives at what is certain to be the story's (un)compelling conclusion, she startles me by clapping her hands together.

"I nearly forgot," she says. "You got something today."

She swings through the screen door and returns with a large cardboard box that she drops at my feet. I lean forward in my chair for a better look. The recipient name scrawled on the mailing label is, rather ambiguously, "The Single Lady."

"I thought for a moment this was mine," Judy says, "until I saw this."

She opens the box and pulls out a sheer blouse with a deep V in the front and back.

"That's my sister's," I say.

"You're sister's something, isn't she?" Judy says, arching an eyebrow at me.

"She sure is." I stand and hug the package to my chest. For the first time all week, I miss home. "I guess I'll go see what other kind of unmentionables are in here."

Judy chuckles and shoos me away with a wave of her hand.

Heather's little care package is indeed filled with all kinds of unmentionables. I place the box on my bed and pull out one scandalous article of clothing after another. But then Heather surprises me. At the bottom of the box I find a rectangular wood crate with "Ginger & Ivory" branded across the front. There are two items inside. The first is a bumper sticker with a quote attributed to Henry David Thoreau. It says: "Go confidently in the direction of your dreams. Live the life you have imagined." The second item is even more wonderful. It is a framed drawing done in the same style as the one Heather did for the catalogue cover. The picture is of two women sitting side by side on the front porch of a Cape Cod house that looks terribly familiar.

I place the frame on my nightstand and look at the two women in the picture again. Heather and me. Sisters.

As I'm packing Heather's clothes back into the box, I notice a pretty white sundress that is relatively modest. I'd never have had the guts to wear something like this in Boise, but then, I'm not in Boise anymore. I slip into the dress and take a look in the mirror. And then, I do a double take.

So this is what confidence looks like.

Not bad.

I grab the bumper sticker Heather gave me and head outside. I've made so many changes this week, why not make one more? I walk to the back of the Corolla and take one last look at the label I've fixed there. "Drive Carefully—90% of People Are Caused by Accidents." Funny, sure, but it's time I touted a new message. I peel the adhesive paper from the Thoreau sticker and place it directly over the old one. Then, I hop in the car. It's time to go in the direction of my dreams.

I drive for a good hour before I finally reach the coast. I take the exit for Huntington Beach and squeeze my car into a skinny stall in a narrow, crowded parking lot. The beach is California embodied. I mean, two blondes are rollerblading down the boardwalk. In bikinis. I wouldn't be surprised if at any minute I spot a bodybuilder hefting a ghetto blaster on his shoulder. It is that classic.

The ocean calls to me. Once I hit the sand, I remove my sandals and let the warm grains massage my bare feet. I walk until the sand becomes nearly solid and the waves lap playfully at my feet. It is late afternoon and the sunlight has fallen onto the water in a million shattered pieces.

The ocean is a revelation. It speaks of endless possibility.

Just before sunset, I reluctantly head back to the parking lot. I have just turned the keys in the ignition when my car suddenly jolts forward. For a half second, I fear the worst and brace myself for the aftershock. But it's not an earthquake. It's an accident. Someone was stupidly trying to back into the empty stall beside me and hit my Corolla instead. The driver pulls forward, away from my bumper, and I crane my neck to get a look at the crash test dummy who just hit me. That's when I catch sight of the wide eyes of Woodsy Owl.

My eyes flash from the bumper sticker to the Nebraska plates. Hannah Montana. I've just been hit by Joe from Omaha.

Joe throws the gear into park and gets out of his car. He walks toward the Corolla and peers through my rolled-down window.

"I'm so sorry," he says. "I misjudged the distance between us and . . ."

Then he sees me. He stops talking and just stares.

"Hi." I get out of the car. He stares some more.

"Sabrina," he finally says.

"What were you trying to do there, Joe?" I motion to my left bumper, which has suffered some considerable damage.

"Park." His cheeks redden and he stares at the ground. "I'm so sorry. It was a mistake."

I look at my crunched bumper. Then I look at Joe. What he just did was unplanned, unintended, and absolutely marvelous. When Joe shyly meets my gaze, I comfort him with something it took me a long time to learn.

"Some mistakes are worth making."

The smile he gives me rivals the glory of the setting sun.

"What are you doing here?" he says.

"I just started school at Caltech. What are you doing here?"

"Trying to complete the list." He pulls a lined piece of paper from his pocket. "My goal is to visit every landmark beach in California before graduation. I started north and am working my way down."

"Okay," I say. "But what are you doing in California?"

"Oh." Joe tucks his adorable list back into his pocket. "I go to UCLA."

"You never told me that."

"You never asked."

Our smile-a-thon is interrupted by an impatient chorus of honking horns. A couple of cars are trying to leave, and Joe's Subaru is blocking the exit.

"I guess I should move my car," Joe says. "You're not going to run away from me again, are you?"

"Not until you give me your insurance info," I say.

I stand by the curb and wait for Joe to park. This time, he manages to maneuver his car into the stall without incident. He rummages through the glove box in his car. Every few seconds he glances toward me, tethering me to him with his eyes.

He emerges from his car and hands me a scrap of paper.

"My insurance information," he says. "I put my number on there too. Just in case."

"Just in case what?"

"Just in case you need to get ahold of me." His face reddens again. "To talk about the claim."

"And what if I want to get a hold of you to talk about something else?"

"Well, then that would be okay too." Joe looks at me with eyes that sparkle like the sea. Then he points toward the pier. "Have you been to Ruby's yet?"

I look at the restaurant at the end of the pier and shake my head.

"Let me buy you dinner."

I accept Joe's offer—not because I'm suddenly bold, but because saying yes feels like the most natural thing in the world. We walk side by side toward the pier, talking easily, our arms occasionally brushing against each other. The sun is setting, casting its long rays around us like a net. I take in everything bound together by this lattice of light—the pervasive scent of salt, the hypnotic roar of the waves, the sensation of Joe's body comfortably close to mine.

When we reach the base of the pier, Joe takes my hand in his. I catch my breath in wonder. Within the space of our clasped hands lies an ocean of possibility.

Life doesn't always go according to plan. That's not necessarily a bad thing. From what I can tell, some of the best things in life just happen, accidentally.

Discussion Questions

1. Calvin tells Sabrina in the Game Shack that he only likes playing games if he wins. In terms of Sabrina and Calvin's relationship, does Calvin ultimately "win"? Do you see him simply as an antagonist or is the role more nuanced?

2. Sabrina describes Thayne Stockett and Jordan Greene as "life-sized Barbie and Ken dolls." These characters represent a type of perfection, albeit a superficial one. How does this conception of perfection differ from the one Sabrina is striving for? How is it similar?

3. Birds appear throughout the novel—both captive and in the wild. How do these portrayals relate to the themes explored in the novel?

4. Is Sabrina a reliable narrator? Is her perception of her parents and siblings justified?

5. Discuss how Sabrina's relationship with her sister Heather changes over the course of the novel. Do you see Heather as a static or dynamic character?

6. Sabrina finally rejects the notion that she has to be perfect to be loved. In what ways is the pursuit of perfection harmful? In what ways is it beneficial?

7. Where do you see Sabrina the summer after her first year of college?

Acknowledgments

Thank you to the entire team at Cedar Fort, especially to Emma Parker for rescuing Sabrina's story from the slush pile and making it shine. Thank you to my parents, Dan and Chris Eldredge, who have encouraged my writing since I was a child, and to my sister, Traci Barnes, for being my first reader and biggest cheerleader. Thank you to my writer friends, particularly Susie Salom and Curtis Moser, for your generous, capacious hearts. Thank you to my children, whose curiosity and sense of wonder inspire me every day. Last, to my husband, Michael "Bubba" Karras, thank you for your support, then and now.

About the Author

Kim Karras has never hired a stalker, although her children often give her the impression she's being watched and followed. After receiving a degree in English from the University of Utah, she jumped into the adventure that is fiction writing, sans safari hat. Kim lives with her husband and three children in Sandy, Utah. You can find her online at kimkarras.blogspot.com.